HEAVY SET HANNAH
AND LIMBER LISA

A BBW (Big Beautiful Woman) Lesbian Erotica

Mickey Gatz

CONTENTS

HEAVY SET
Hannah
AND
Limber
Lisa
A BBW (Big Beautiful Woman) Lesbian Erotica
MICKEY GATZ

CHAPTER 1

The sunshine, reaching through the sheer white curtains, flickered on Hannah's face. Wrapped up in the blankets, the girl creased her brows and rolled over, turning her back at the window. Dozing off, she continued breathing heavily and stretched the coverlet up to her chin, digging her face into the soft pillow. But suddenly, a screeching sound of the alarm ringing pierced the silence, making Hannah turn around and slam her palm on the phone, silencing it. Sighing, she sat up, rubbing her eyes and yawning like a newly awoken baby. As the realization of starting her day arrived, she growled and put her head back.

"I don't want to get up," she muttered, staring at the ceiling.

She had to endure one more day of the mocking, whispers, insulting remarks, and loud giggling. The endless bullying had become an inseparable part of her everyday life, and after getting out of bed, all she could think about was the time she'd return to it - her room, the safe place where no one judged her, where she was alone with her dreams, in her little, pink bubble.

"Hannah?" suddenly, the husky yet gentle voice reached her, and Hanna looked at the slightly open door. "Are you awake?"

A smile formed across Hannah's lips. She wasn't alone, and she had someone who helped her drag her feet through the day - Lisa, her roommate. Because of her, Hannah managed to live a somewhat normal life, forget the offensive comments thrown at her and enjoy her college life. Not entirely, but without Lisa, it would be a lot harder as she was her only friend.

"Yeah, I am!" Hanna replied and crawled out of the blankets, almost staggering into the kitchen.

The fresh, crisp air was coming through the open windows,

fluttering Lisa's hair as she stood at the stove, cracking eggs into a frying pan.

"Good morning," she turned around, broadly smiling at Hannah, shining her white teeth under her full, red lips.

Looking at her, Hannah couldn't help but smile back.

"Omelets will be ready in a second!" said Lisa and continued stirring the eggs.

Her clear voice, ringing like bells, woke up Hannah's sleepy mind, and she sat at the table, gazing at her roommate. The long, baggy t-shirt that Lisa wore hung on her lean body like a sack, revealing her long, bare legs. Still, Hannah thought that whatever Lisa wore, she always looked beautiful. And she wasn't wrong. Even the most basic clothes adorned Lisa's fit, well-built body, slightly muscular from training. As she stood, making the breakfast, the yellow beams of sunshine danced on her honey-blonde curls, falling on her shoulders, sparkling as if covered with dew. The long eyelashes shadowed her blue eyes, deep like an ocean, and her lips, smiling, looked carved out of marble. Hannah wondered how could a normal person have such perfectly balanced features.

She looks like a fairy out of a fantasy world; the thought crossed her mind as she stared at Lisa.

Suddenly, she turned around, chuckling as dimples formed on her soft cheeks like little half-moons.

"Why are you looking at me like that?" Lisa asked, giggling.

"Oh, I just zoned out," Hanna muttered and looked down as redness spread on her face.

"The breakfast is ready!" Lisa exclaimed and flopped the omelets on the plates, next to neatly cut tomatoes. Her creamy white hands flexibility moved as she poured orange juice into the glasses and put them on the table.

"Tell me how it is," she let out and sniffled the plate, her pointy nose scrunching. "It smells good, right?"

Hannah took a bite with the fork and moaned from pleasure.

"Ah, it's amazing!" she exclaimed. "You are a real cook, Lisa!"

"Really?" Lisa's eyes started glimmering from delight, and her lips opened as she tasted her coup too. "I really am good."

Both laughed, and as Hannah felt her face hurting from smiling, she thought that no one could make her laugh except Lisa.

While eating, Lisa looked at the clock, ticking on the wall.

"We gotta hurry up," she said and stuffed her mouth with the rest of the meal, trying to contain laughter as Hannah did the same.

"I'm gonna go take a shower," mumbled Hannah with her full cheeks and jumped up from the chair.

"Okay, be quick!" Lisa said as she scurried into her room.

Walking into the bathroom, Hannah turned the shower on, and while taking off her pajamas, she caught a glimpse of herself in the mirror. Listening to the water pattering, Hannah drew closer to her reflection, glaring at it. The girl in the mirror did the same, and as she stared more, the scowl on her face grew deeper, wrinkles forming on her forehead from anger. Disappointment and frustration made Hannah's mouth bent downward, and she furrowed her brows as if she was seeing herself for the first time. Despite living with her body for 21 years, Hannah hadn't learned to love it. Every time she looked into the mirror, she felt like she was looking at a stranger as if she was someone she wasn't supposed to be. As though the universe had made a mistake and given her a wrong body, a body that no one liked, that no one wanted, that everyone despised. As if Hannah got the leftover body that others rejected, threw out in the garbage, and the universe had nothing left but the worst, spurn one for her.

But no one hated Hannah as Hannah herself. That's why she avoided looking in the mirror, but now, as the hot water fogged up the glass, she couldn't help but stare with disgust at her blurry reflection.

Her short, pitch-black hair hardly covered her ears, revealing her thick neck. Her white, pallid skin was marked with spots and darker patches, some birthmarks, some scars, some pimples. The black bra covered her full chest that almost touched her round arms.

Hannah ran her short, meaty fingers through her frizzy hair, sighing and running her eyes over her body once again. The rotund legs were put together, and her panties clutched around her shapeless waist.

The more she stared, the more her caramel brown eyes got filled with resentment. She pursed her parched lips and rubbed her face as if trying to erase it. Even though she had a small, well-shaped nose, elongated, foxy brows, and sharp jaws, Hannah couldn't see them, and if she did, she considered them ugly too.

She peered at the flat weight scale standing next to the door. Biting her lower lip, Hannah contemplated standing on it. Even though she knew the number would disappoint her as always, she still put one foot on the scale, squeezing her eyes shut as if when she'd open them, she'd see what she wished for.

But when she opened her eyes, staring right between her feet at the number brightening in red, Hannah felt tears rushing, burning her eyes.

"300 pounds," she let out. "Still."

One tear escaped, rolling down her cheek, making her feel like boiling water had been dribbled down her face. Her insides were burning just like her eyes, from pain and disappointment that kept growing roots deep in her heart.

Wiping off the tear, Hannah swallowed the ball stuck in her throat and took off the underwear, stepping into the shower. The water, wetting her hair and sliding down her skin, calmed her down a little. Hannah closed her eyes, gliding her palms on her head, putting it back and trying to stop thinking about herself, cloud her mind with something peaceful, something that would bring serenity to her agitated, hurt soul.

"Lisa," whisper left Hannah's mouth.

She was that someone who could fog her mind with peace and quiet. Everything would be alright as long as Lisa was by her side.

"Hannah, we're going to be late!" she heard Lisa's voice calling from outside and turned the shower off.

"I'm coming!" Hannah replied and wrapped the towel around her body, clenching the doorknob to open but stepped back in a second. Lisa was in the living room, and if Hannah went out with the towel only covering part of her body, revealing her legs and arms, Lisa would see her. Hannah couldn't let herself go out like that even though Lisa had seen her naked many times as they were childhood friends. And she had never, not once, made fun of Hannah. Still, Hannah couldn't go outside without putting on the robe that covered her whole body, not leaving an inch unhidden, showing only her hands and face.

"Come on, Hannah, you know we'll be in trouble," said Lisa with a smile as Hannah rushed out of the bathroom into her room.

"Yeah, sorry, I'll be right out," Hannah responded and closed the door.

She opened the wardrobe, throwing out the clothes and putting them on - a black baggy shirt stretched to her ankles and two sizes bigger jeans. Lastly, she put a black choker necklace, decorated with a silver hoop, around her neck. She had no time to do her usual Gothic, dark makeup, so after slipping her feet into the high-platformed leather shoes, Hannah barged into the living room.

"Finally," Lisa chuckled and grabbed her bag, throwing Hannah's to her. "Let's go."

They left the apartment, and Lisa locked it with a key, shoving it in her pocket. They were renting a two-bedroom apartment, a few-minutes-long walk from the college.

As they ran down the stairs, Lisa put her hand over Hannah's shoulder, stepping out in the streets.

"What are your plans today?" Lisa asked, her face beaming into a wide smile, the half-moons forming at the ends of it.

What plan would she have? Lisa knew the answer, but Hannah felt grateful that she still asked.

"Nothing," Hannah replied and shrugged.

"Then will you come to my game after classes?"

"Of course!" Hannah exclaimed. "How can I miss it!"

"Great! You are a real friend, Hannah! You never miss a play," she said, kissing Hannah on the cheek. As Lisa's lips touched her skin, she felt warmth pouring into her.

The sun spread its light generously, dying the surroundings in bright orange as Hannah and Lisa walked down the street. People crowded it, everyone rushing somewhere, passing by the girls with short, quick steps. The irritating sound of traffic, honking, and angry insults, thrown out of the open car windows lanced the air. The cars, trying to inch their way through the gridlock, looked like beetles crushing into their hole in the ground.

Despite the stuffy, hot air that made her back covered in sweat, the earsplitting honking, and rushing people jolting her every second, Hannah still enjoyed the bright morning, especially when Lisa was next to her.

Suddenly someone cuffed her.

"Step aside, fatty!" the man shouted and hurried forward, not looking back at Hannah, whose heart shrunk from pain.

"Hey! You, asshole!" Lisa shouted at the man, but he was already too far, and the noise overshadowed the girl's voice.

"Dickhead," Lisa mumbled and looked at Hannah, who was looking down. She was already used to hearing insults from total strangers. At first, she used to start crying, but throughout the years, she learned to bottle her feelings up and silently struggle without showing it. She only let them out when she was alone, in her room, wrapped up in blankets. Only then did her tears wet the pillow, and her hands clenched its edges.

But real mocking would start when they'd step into the college yard. And Hannah dreaded it. She feared stepping into the gate like a kid fears a night monster.

Lisa noticed Hannah's eyes avoiding looking at people as they drew closer to the college, and she gripped her hand.

"Everything will be okay," she whispered in Hannah's ear. "Ignore those dumbasses."

Hannah forced a smile and tried to think about Lisa's hand, holding hers and nothing else.

But it was hard. As soon as they walked through the massive metal gates and stepped into the yard, the heads turned toward them. The students, lined up along the path into groups, threw judgmental glances toward Hannah. Some holding books, some clutching bags, some scrolling through their phones, some whispering tittle-tattle - everyone fixed their eyes on Hannah.

Overwhelmed by the attention, Hannah looked down at her shoes, feeling how Lisa gripped her hand tightly that had started sweating from anxiety.

The college wasn't big, and it wasn't hard for the five hundred students to know a lot about each other. Hannah had thought that studying in a smaller college would be easier, but she had been mistaken. In a little group, the secrets and gossips spread in a second.

Lisa and Hannah walked on the path, paved with white stones, under the broad branches of pine trees, toward the three-story, red-bricked building. They could hear murmurs and quiet snickers as they'd pass a group of students.

"Yo, you dike lard-ass!" a voice reached them, followed by snickers and chortles.

Hannah had come out as a lesbian in high school, and since then, she had never hidden her sexuality. But little did she know how much struggle it would bring. Sometimes Hannah wondered that maybe she should've concealed her true self. But as soon as she'd bring up the subject of masking her sexuality by showing interest in boys, Lisa would change her mind.

"Behaving the way others want you to behave is the weakest thing a person can do," she would say. After spending so many years by her side, Hannah saw how real and honest Lisa was, unapologetically revealing her true self and enjoying it. Lisa was her role model, and Hannah decided that she had to stay authentic despite the struggle. Being someone, she wasn't would put her in much more pain.

Hannah stopped and shrugged, squeezing her eyes shut, trying not to let the anger wash over her.

But she knew Lisa wasn't going to ignore the bullies. Hannah grabbed her hand to stop Lisa, but the girl clenched her jaws and turned around.

The group of bullies sat on the bench - three boys and two girls. As Lisa turned toward them, their smirks grew broader, and the boy who had called Hannah calmly folded his arms, leaning on the back of the chair with a confident look on his face as if satisfied that he had managed to irk someone.

With tightened fists and furrowed brows, Lisa walked up near them as Hannah looked back, seeing how she pointed at the boy with disgust bursting out of her eyes.

"Nick, You piece of shit," Lisa said through her clenched teeth. "Don't you have anything else to do other than speak nothing but hate?"

Nick scoffed as his lips curved upward. Glancing at his friends, amused by the show, Nick tutted.

"Why should I?" he asked and peered at Hannah. "When I can have real fun by just looking at her."

Hannah stared at them silently, motionlessly. She was happy that Lisa was standing up for her but annoyed that she couldn't do it herself.

"Go fuck yourself, Nick," said Lisa and walked further from him as if avoiding a garbage can. "Isn't that all you do anyway? Since no one wants to fuck you."

Nick's features slackened, and his smile vanished. Soon students who had been watching them started giggling and peeking toward him. Embarrassed, Nick looked down before spitting out.

"Shut up!" he yelled at the students.

With a winner's smile, Lisa turned around, walking back to Hannah, who, just like others, was scoffing, enjoying Nick's frustration.

As they continued walking to the college, Hannah, unable to contain the amazement, whispered to Lisa.

"That was so cool! How can you be so," she paused, searching for the right word as Lisa watched her with a smile. "So, confident?!"

Lisa put her arm around Hannah.

"I can be everything when my best friend needs me," she

said and kissed her cheek.

Hannah forgot about the recent incident and the offensive words as Lisa walked right beside her. She felt secure in her company as if nothing would hurt her, or she'd be able to endure every hardship as long as Lisa held her hand.

They went into the building, full of students hurrying to the classrooms. Hannah liked the white walls and big, bright windows. She liked the interior, also, the professors and the subjects. It was the students that ruined her college years.

"What do you have now?" Lisa asked and scrolled through her phone to find the schedule.

"Creative strategy," said Hannah and noticed the time on Lisa's phone. "What about you?"

"Statistics," Lisa said and groaned. "Ugh, I hate this subject."

Hannah noticed the time on Lisa's phone.

"It's already 9!" she exclaimed. "We gotta go!"

"Come on!" Lisa took her hand, running into the hall.

They giggled while rushing to the classrooms. As Hannah reached hers, Lisa let go of her hand.

"I'll see you at lunch!" she said and waved at her. "Go, go, or Ms. Miller will scold you."

Lisa grimaced, mocking the professor and making Hannah laugh. She waved again before running up the stairs and disappearing on the second floor.

Hannah opened the door, and everyone turned their heads toward her. The professor, standing at the board, stopped talking and pointed at the desks.

"Sorry, Ms. Miller," Hannah apologized and walked to the desk, taking her seat.

The professor's face twisted just like Lisa had imitated, and as she turned around, Hannah covered her mouth with a hand, unable to contain quiet laughter.

*

The sun reached its zenith on the clear sky. The surroundings were sinking into burnt orange light as Hannah left the classroom, looking around for Lisa.

As the crowd of students came out of the class, she was pushed to move toward being squeezed into the group.

Hannah's heart started galloping, and her pulse raised. Sweat drops started covering her back as the students kept getting louder, moving without knowing how they cuffed and jerked Hannah.

Suddenly she felt a touch on her shoulder and looked back, seeing Lisa. Hannah's pulse turned normal, and her heart stopped racing as Lisa smiled at her and took her arm.

"How was the class?" Lisa asked and helped Hannah separate from the noisy crowd.

"Okay," Hannah replied.

"I'm so hungry," Lisa rubbed her stomach. "I could eat a horse."

Hannah laughed as they headed toward the cafeteria. Hannah peeked toward Lisa, wearing a simple black shirt and tight jeans. Looking at her lean torso, Hannah wondered how she could have so much appetite.

They walked into the cafeteria. The students had already filled the tables, blabbering, laughing, and eating. Hannah and Lisa took the trays, filled them with food, and walked down through the aisles of tables.

They discerned two girls, holding trays of food, walking toward them, and heading to the table. Their long, styled hair fell to their waist, the short, colorful skirts clasping their thighs, the deep cleavage and bare neck would draw anyone's attention. Their faces, covered in thick layers of makeup, charmingly smiling, revealed their confidence. The girls knew they were pretty, and they knew it was a weapon. And they used it.

Hannah sighed, seeing the girls walking in high heels, with their chins up, and took her eyes off of them.

I wish I were as confident as them; the thought lanced her mind.

But she knew that confidence came along with beauty, and without beauty, they were nothing. Still, she dreamed of their hair, their long, slim legs, and clear skin. Every time she'd look at the girls, pain pierced her heart, and she felt like she was being stabbed. The mental pain was so intense that it turned into physical.

"Isn't she the one who called you ugly?" Suddenly Lisa's voice dispersed her thoughts.

Lisa pointed at the girl, with dark hair and fair skin, walking to Lisa's right.

"Yeah," Hannah mumbled and waved her hand. "It's okay. I'm used to it, you know."

Hannah told the truth, but she wouldn't have if she knew what Lisa would do.

After a few seconds, as the girls drew closer to them, Lisa, as if checking her phone, spread her hand and pushed the tray in the brunette girl's hand. The tray flipped, and the food - a glass of juice and salad- splashed on her shirt. The colors of the meal immediately stained her white top, and the girl gasped, looking down at herself and then at Lisa, her jaw dropped from shock.

"Oh, sorry," Lisa said with fake empathy. "I didn't see you."

Before the girl could reply, Lisa turned around, grabbing Hannah's hand, and walked past the girl, still standing frozen. The students, startled by the sudden commotion, gawked at them. Some had even pulled out their phones, taking photos of the victim.

Lisa and Hannah sat at the corner table, and Lisa took her hamburger, taking a big bite.

"Why did you do that?" Hannah asked, her pupils dilating from surprise.

"She deserved it," Lisa winked and continued eating, as if she was eating alone, the ketchup smudging all over her mouth.

Looking at her, Hannah couldn't help but chuckle.

"You shouldn't do stuff like that."

"When she stops being a bitch, I'll stop humiliating her too," Lisa said with a stuffed mouth.

Hannah shook her head, partly disapproving of her friend's behavior, partly enjoying it. She started slowly eating, with small bites, covering her mouth while chewing. Hannah always felt awkward while eating, as if afraid to give people reason to call her a pig, which they often did. On the other hand, Lisa never minded if others saw that she ate like a little, starving animal.

As Lisa gulped down coca-cola, she creased her brows.

"Aren't you uncomfortable in that outfit?" she asked. "It's so hot."

Hannah looked down at her long-sleeved shirt and shrugged.

"Not really," she uttered.

"It's summer," Lisa smiled. "You should let your skin breathe. And ignore everyone who says something mean. They are rotten inside."

Hannah's lips spit as she tried to smile but failed. Hannah knew Lisa was right, but her advice wasn't always so easy to follow.

Hannah's last class ended in two hours, and she grabbed her bag, rushing to Lisa's game. She felt relieved as if a heavyweight had been lifted from her chest. She let out a sigh while walking down the hallway. Finally, the classes had ended, and she could spend the rest of the day in peace.

The clouds drifted by on the blue sky as the sun slowly approached the horizon and its shine faded. Silence shrouded around the college as everyone had left for the basketball game. Hannah, too, hastened her steps, impatient to arrive before Lisa would show up.

In a few minutes, she stepped into the room, full of the students, lined up on the long chairs encircling the basketball court. Everyone was agitated, and the excitement had piled up in tension as the crowd got impatient.

Hannah took her seat, watching the cheerleaders dancing with flashy skirts on catchy, blaring music. As they ended their performance, the girls created a path by standing in a line to the left and right of the entrance door where the players would come out from.

The players started running out, throwing air kisses to

the audience that kept cheering and welcoming them with loud whistles and claps. But the ovation grew even louder as Lisa - the star player showed up. With a broad, confident smile, Lisa ran out, waving at her fans and nodding in gratitude as they screamed and applauded.

Hannah, too, stood up, clapping. As Lisa saw her, she waved and winked.

In a few minutes, the game started. Lisa moved so effortlessly as if not even touching the floor but flying above it. Her flexible body slid through the opponents, cutting her way through the crowd, running as fast as some kind of insect. Her legs didn't seem to get tired as they hastened every second.

As Lisa lanced the air, jumped, and threw the ball that flipped right through the basket, people couldn't contain gasp of amazement.

Hannah watched full of support, clapping every time Lisa made a smart move or brought a score to her team. The red short and tight top fitted her perfectly as her curls, put up in a ponytail, bounced as she'd jump.

The game ended with Lisa's team winning. People saw them off with waving banners and shouting "victory" as usual. Hannah smiled at Lisa as she waved before disappearing from the court with the sound of ovation following her.

"She won," Hannah murmured, her eyes glimmering from joy. "Once again."

*

As Lisa waved at the screaming audience, she ran inside, headed to the locker room. Beats of sweat covered her forehead, and her clothes, as well as her hair, looked soaked. Lisa couldn't wait to run into the shower room, but as she approached the locker room, one of the players ran out, dragging her inside.

"Come on; we want to thank you," she said to Lisa.

Lisa sighed with a smile as the team welcomed her with a group hug. Everyone wrapped their arms around each other, slightly rocking back and forth.

"We are one!" they yelled together before scattering.

Lisa opened her locker, taking out the towel and clothes, and was about to walk into the shower when a voice coming from her back stopped her.

"Hey, Lisa, wait a minute." Turning around, Lisa saw one of her team members smiling at her.

"Yes, Gemma?" Lisa replied. Gemma tapped the towel on her face to dry the sweat and looked up at Lisa.

"I'm throwing a party tonight to celebrate our victory," she said. "The girls will be there too," she pointed at the team. "Will you come?"

Lisa peered toward the girls, engrossed in chatter, and hesitated for a second. She didn't want to leave Hannah, but also, it had been a while since she'd been to a party.

"Can I bring my friend?" she asked.

"Sure!" Gemma nodded. "Bring whoever you want."

"Then, sure, I'll be there," Lisa smiled.

"Great. I'll text you the address."

As Gemma got back to her locker, Lisa went into the shower, letting the cool water wash away her exhaustion. She loosely dropped her hands, listening to the girls pattering about the party, and wondered if she'd be able to convince Hannah to go with her.

Clasping the towel around her body, Lisa came out, back into the locker room, now partly empty. After changing and blow-drying her hair, Lisa grabbed her bag.

"Good game, everyone," she said to the team members and walked outside.

As she stepped out in the college yard, she discerned Hannah sitting at the table with a book spread in front of her, her eyes hastily running from one edge of the paper to the other, hands neatly placed like a schoolkid. Seeing her, Lisa slapped her forehead from realization.

Shit, I forgot to give her the key to our apartment, she thought.

The sun had already sunk behind the horizon, and the streetlights shone in dim yellow, illuminating Hannah's face, tense from concentration. Lisa released she had been waiting since the end of the game and felt terrible for forgetting about the key. But as she stood there, watching her friend, Lisa knew Hannah would still wait for her even if she had the key so that they could walk back home together.

"Hey," Lisa approached her. "Sorry, I forgot about the key."

Hannah looked up and closed the book, putting it in her bag.

"Key?" she asked and thought for a while. "Oh, the apartment key. I didn't even remember that. I was waiting for you."

A smile rose to Lisa's lips as they began strolling down the path.

"Thank you," she said and paused a little, afraid of Hannah's reaction. "One of the team members invited me to a party tonight. Don't you wanna come?"

Hannah shrugged and hid her neck in her shoulders. Pursing her lips, Hannah shook her head.

"There's no place for me there," she said with an awkward, forced chuckle. "It's your team."

"There will be others too," said Lisa, noticing how Hannah avoided looking at her. "It will be fun. We'll drink! The girls are kind. You'll like them."

Hannah sighed, but before she could deny it, Lisa grabbed her hands, jumping in front of her and staring into her eyes.

"Please, just a few hours," she let out, begging. "We need to go out once in a while. It's our chance."

Hannah licked her lips, hesitating.

"Please," Lisa kept on.

"Okay," Hannah nodded and laughed. "If you insist."

"Yes!" Lisa clapped and put her arm over Hannah's shoulder. "Maybe you'll like one of the girls and get yourself a girlfriend."

Hannah fell silent. Little did Lisa know that the one Hannah had been in love with for years was her.

As they stepped into the apartment, Hannah went into her room to change for the party, and so did Lisa. She never thought a lot about an outfit, and as she opened her wardrobe, she took out the first shirt she landed her eyes on. Putting it on, Lisa let her hair down and glided a clear lip gloss on her lips. Only a few minutes had passed, and she was ready. Waiting for Hannah, she flopped on her bed, scrolling through her phone. The white bedsheets matched the light blue wallpaper and open shelves with a few plants on them. The minimalistic interior reflected Lisa's personality.

As fifteen minutes passed, Lisa knocked on Hannah's door.

"Hey, did you fall asleep?" Lisa asked, even though she knew why Hannah was still not ready. She was aware her friend was insecure, and the anxiety intensified every time she was about to meet new people.

Hannah slowly opened the door and peeked through the gap with sad eyes.

"I don't know what to wear," she mumbled.

"Let me in, and I'll help," Lisa chirped.

Hannah opened the door, and Lisa walked inside, sprawling on the black bedsheets. The dark grey wallpaper created a gloomy atmosphere, but Lisa had never mentioned anything, respecting her friend's choice, as it was Hannah's taste: dark colors, Gothic style.

"Let me see what you have," putting her chin on her hands, Lisa said.

Hannah opened the wardrobe.

"Oh, that green hoodie looks cool," Lisa let out, pointing at it.

"Don't you think it's too? I don't know," Hannah muttered. "Not for a party."

"Absolutely not!" said Lisa and stood up. "Put that on. I'll wait outside."

After a few minutes, Hannah showed up with the hoodie on, black shadows around her eyes, and dark purple lipstick.

"You look so cool!" Lisa exclaimed and spread her hand. "Let's go."

They took a taxi, and during the ride, Lisa noticed how Hannah kept biting her lips and picking her skin on her fingers from nervousness, staring through the window as if she wanted the road to stretch longer.

Lisa took her hand, making Hannah look at her.

"Everything will be fine," she whispered. "Let loose and just have fun."

Hannah nodded, smiling. "I'll try."

As they arrived and rang the doorbell, the door opened, and Gemma appeared with a plastic cup in her hand.

"Oh, welcome, welcome!" she said.

"You already drunk?" Lisa asked, laughing.

"A little," the girl said and led them inside.

The two-story house was full of youth, dancing to blasting music and drinking from one glass after another.

Taking Hannah's hand, Lisa walked to her group of friends.

"This is Hannah," she said to everyone. "My best friend and my roommate."

"Hi, Hannah!" the students welcomed her, and one of them shoved glasses of alcohol to their hands. "Let's drink!"

Lisa and Hannah shared a look, and Lisa winked at her before gulping down the drink. Hannah, too, encouraged by her friend, put her head back and swelled the alcohol.

The students clapped and filled the glasses again. Suddenly the music grew louder, and the lights switched into disco ball imitation, brightening the room with small, silver spots of light spinning around the walls.

Everyone left the cups, joining the dancing crowd. Lisa took Hannah's hand, pushing her toward the dance floor. As Hannah hesitated, she said into her ear.

"No one's watching."

Hannah looked around, seeing the sweaty youth immersed into the music, dancing as if there was no tomorrow.

As Lisa pulled her again, Hannah obeyed her and stepped into the agitated adolescents, letting the ecstasy take over them. Following the rhythm of the music, Lisa held Hannah's hands, dancing with her. As she saw her friend closing her eyes, feeling the music and swaying her hips, Lisa realized that for the first time in a long while, Hannah was finally having fun.

CHAPTER 2

The sun blazed down on the college yard, full of students. Hannah sat on a bench with a book spread in her lap while the music blasting out her earphones overshadowed the loud chatter of the students. She couldn't concentrate on the book, thinking about Lisa and when she'd show up. Being alone wasn't unfamiliar for Hannah; on the contrary, she enjoyed her own company where no one judged her or gave away unsolicited advice. But now, as the people kept passing by her while throwing glances at her, Hannah couldn't wait to jump up and rush home. But she had promised Lisa to meet up after the classes, so she kept enduring the struggle on which some might have laughed, but for Hannah, it was equal to being skinned alive.

Suddenly she heard a voice lancing through her music, calling her name. Hannah smiled, recognizing the voice that felt like home. Putting her head up, Hannah's smile faded in a second, melting like snow under sunshine. Lisa was walking with her usual steady, long steps, waving at Hannah with a broad smile. But she wasn't alone; a boy walked next to her.

Hannah's felt like her heart jumped up to her throat, getting stuck in there so she couldn't swallow or make a sound.

Who is he? Train of thought started piercing her mind. *I've seen him before. Isn't he a football player? Why are Lisa and he walking together?*

Lisa and the boy soon approached her, and startled, Hannah almost threw the book back in her bag.

"Hey, Hannah, this is Chet," Lisa smiled, pointing at the boy and then putting her arm over Hannah's shoulder. "This is my best friend."

"Nice to meet you, Hannah," Chet smiled, shining his perfectly straight teeth, spreading his hand.

"Nice to meet you too," Hannah shook his hand, feeling the strength in it.

Chet straightened his back, putting his hands in the pockets. His muscular body looked about ten inches taller than Hannah's. The long arms and legs were bulky from training, and the shape of abs on his torso was visible throughout the tight, white shirt. His chocolate brown hair shone under the sunlight, and the thick brows emphasized his deep-set, dark eye. He was handsome, undoubtedly.

Hannah looked at Lisa with confused eyes. Her friend smiled playfully and gazed at Chet.

"We are dating," she said, and a smile split her lips from ear to ear.

Hit by the unexpected news, Hannah lost the ability to talk. Her pupils widened into discs and set on Lisa as if still not believing what she had heard.

Lisa laughed at Hannah's reaction and let go of her, now clinging to Chet's arm. The veins bulged under his tanned skin.

"Aren't you happy?" Lisa laughed and looked at Chet with dreamy eyes. The boy smiled too, gently brushing Lisa's hair out of her face.

"Yes, of course, I am," Hannah mumbled and forced a smile.

While the light wrapped around the couple, soaking them in golden yellow, Lisa and Chet looked like a perfect couple - a beautiful girl and a handsome boy. But the more Hannah watched, the more painful it got. She felt like her heart was shattering into pieces, and even if she tried her best, she could never piece it back together.

It was so sudden that Hannah couldn't feel anything other than distress and confusion. Lisa had never mentioned him before, and Hannah hadn't seen her talking to Chet. What if Lisa didn't even know him well enough? What if he hurt her feelings?

"Wanna go to a cafe?" Chet's low voice interrupted her racing thoughts.

Before Hannah could answer, Lisa grabbed her arm and squealed. "Yeah, I'm so hungry!"

Chet chuckled and spread his hand at Lisa, who was still clinging onto Hannah. As Chet stood, waiting for Lisa, Hannah sensed that he was giving her an ultimatum - she had to choose between him and her friend.

Looking at Hannah, sparkle died in Lisa's eyes, and Hannah knew that she sensed the atmosphere too. Still, Lisa let go of Hannah, putting her hand in Chet's, who entangled his fingers into hers. The couple started strolling in front of Hannah as she followed them like an obedient puppy.

I had a foreboding as soon as I woke up today, thought Hannah. *And turns out, I sensed right.*

They reached the nearby cafe, full of students with barely empty seats. As they went inside, Lisa turned at Hannah.

"I'll go take a seat before others do," she said. "You and Chet bring the food."

She slipped through the crowd, sitting at the table facing a wide window. Left alone with Chet, Hannah felt the awkwardness putting shackles on her movements. She hid her hands in the pockets and shrugged even though the heat piled up in the cafe could melt a candle.

Chet pursed his lips, seemingly displeased by being alone next to Hannah.

"So, have you and Lisa been friends for a long time?" he asked and peeked toward the line as though not interested in what he had asked.

"Yeah, since kindergarten," Hannah replied.

"That's a long time," Chet said. His lips curved up every time he spoke as if unsuccessfully trying to hide his cynicism.

Three girls passed by them, giving Chet a second look with cunning smiles. Pleased with the attention, Chet ran his fingers through his thick, curly hair and put his chin up. Hannah had never seen someone whose self-confidence turned into narcissism so obviously. She wondered why did Lisa like him, what she found in common with a guy like Chet?

Maybe I'm judging too hard; Hannah stopped herself. I don't even know him.

"Finally, it's my turn," Chet sighed and opened his wallet, not even looking at the cashier. "Three coffees and six doughnuts."

Suddenly he looked back at Hannah. "Do you want more?"

Hannah felt her blood boiling from anger and bit her lower lip.

"No," she said through her clenched teeth.

Chet paid and took one tray without thanking the cashier, handing another tray to Hannah. As the boy walked in front of her, Hannah fought the urge to flip the tray of coffee over his head.

Lisa smiled as they approached and emptied the seat for Chet to sit down next to her.

"Mmm," Lisa moaned, chewing the doughnut.

Hannah sipped the coffee. Chet put the coffee in front of him and folded his arms, seemingly not planning to drink it. His every move seemed controlled, almost robotic.

"How did you meet?" Hannah asked.

"There was this gathering of football and basketball players," said Lisa with her cheeks full. "I met him there. And I was totally stunned!"

"And when was this?" Hannah asked.

"A week ago," Lisa hesitated as though ashamed she hadn't mentioned it to Hannah before. Embarrassed, Lisa looked down, avoiding Hannah's gaze, who now didn't hide her confusion.

"So, you've known each other for only a week," she said. "That's a short time."

"Yes, but you don't have to wait when you see your true love," Chet smiled and put his hand over Lisa's shoulder. Hannah loved when Lisa did the same to her, but now watching Chet's meaty arm around her friend, Hannah felt like Chet considered Lisa nothing but his possession.

True love, huh? Hannah thought and contained a skeptical scoff. *What does he know about true love? The love I have for Lisa is a true love that had lasted for so long.*

However hard it was, Hannah admitted that she was jealous. Beside this star boy with a fit body that every girl adored, Hannah stood no chance. Of course, Lisa would be charmed by him and confuse love with simple attraction.

Still, Hannah wondered how couldn't Lisa see how self-centered Chet was. Just ten minutes were enough for Hannah to see the boy's true self because she wasn't blinded by his gleaming skin and shiny hair, unlike Lisa, who saw nothing behind the facade. Hannah was sure that Chet just wanted Lisa by his side to brag about having a basketball champion and one of the most beautiful girls as a girlfriend.

"How was your day?" Lisa asked Hannah, biting the third doughnut.

"Babe, don't speak with your mouth full," Chet said, his irritation poorly masked by a thin smile.

Lisa mumbled something from discomfort and swallowed. Straightening her back, Lisa carefully wiped her lips and rested her hands in her lap. Hannah's eyes followed her movements, realizing how unusual it was for Lisa to act like a shy lady. Hannah loved Lisa's unashamed way of eating and other wild habits, but they seemed to suppress next to Chet.

"It was okay," Hannah replied, still gazing at Lisa, who sat quietly. "History professor skipped the class."

"That's great," said Lisa, but her mind seemed to be flying far away.

Chet looked down at his watch and exhaled, standing up.

"I have to go, I have a practice," he said with a lower tone as if sad he had to leave, but Hannah saw right through that artificial, robotic smile. He couldn't wait to get Hannah out of his sight. "Will you come, babe?"

Lisa looked up and then back at Hannah. They always went home together and had lunch before doing homework while sprawled on the sofa, which often shifted into afternoon naps and abandoned books.

Hannah discerned sparkles of guilt in Lisa's eyes as if she was apologizing wordlessly. After a second, she stood up, holding

Chet's hand.

"You have the key, right?" she asked Hannah, and when she nodded, Lisa waved. "See you tonight."

"See you," Hannah muttered, seeing the couple walking out of the cafe. Chet glanced back, his eyes piercing Hannah as if flaunting his victory. Hannah realized that it was a competition between him and her about who Lisa would choose in the end.

Left alone, Hannah sighed and drooped her shoulders, digging her head in her arms and staying motionless for a few seconds as though taking everything in - Lisas's boyfriend, the sudden changes in her behavior, Chet's concealed personality. It was too much, even for Hannah, who was used to dealing with a lot simultaneously.

Putting her head up, she set her eyes on the two doughnuts that Lisa hadn't touched and been melting in the stuffy air, twirling inside the cafe. Hannah heard her stomach rumbling and clenched it, afraid others would hear it too. Looking around, she realized no one was watching. She hadn't eaten since morning, and the news about Lisa had made her appetite vanish entirely. But now, as she was back to earth, drained from the feelings washing over her - jealousy, sadness, surprise - she felt like she had never been so hungry. Her stomach was shrinking and her throat turning numb. Seizing one of the doughnuts, Hannah gaped her mouth, taking a huge bite. As the mass of partly-melted chocolate slipped down her throat, Hannah exhaled, feeling herself in her body again. Suddenly, from the corner of her eye, she noticed eyes gawking at her. Turning her head, Hannah saw a little girl about five years old with two ponytails staring at her with horrified curiosity. Hannah realized that she had forgotten how people used to react when she ate. With her temples throbbing from humiliation and frustration, Hannah coughed and grabbed her bag, hurrying out of the cafe with short, quick steps.

*

The sun had sunk behind the horizon; the burnt orange

light had shifted into the darkness that shrouded the city. Hannah lay on the sofa, trying to read a book while peering toward her phone. She couldn't calm her anxiety down. It was past midnight, and Lisa still wasn't home. Hannah sighed, turning to her side and tossing the book away, grabbing the phone. Her eyes fixed on its screen and the number 12:05. Five slowly changed into six; six changed into seven, and Hannah still stared at it. She felt like the time passed dreadfully slow when Lisa wasn't by her side. As if Lisa was the only one coloring Hannah's dull, gray life and without her, everything lost its meaning, taste, becoming too unbearable.

Hannah inhaled so deeply that her chest expanded. She felt something pinching her heart, realizing it was a result of remembering Lisa with Chet. Just the image of the couple fleshing by in her mind made Hannah ache from pain. She put on music, trying to shake her head off of the depressing thoughts but instead, the image got clearer.

"Something's wrong with me," Hannah rubbed her face. "I shouldn't be feeling so sad. Lisa is happy. Isn't that everything I want?"

But still, Hannah couldn't fight the foreboding that Chet would break Lisa's heart. That he wasn't what Lisa thought he was, and it was just a character Chet was playing in front of others.

Suddenly the door opened, and Lisa walked in, staggering, with face red as if someone had splashed crimson paint on it. She was smiling, and her knees kept wiggling.

"Oh, are you drunk?!" Hannah stood up, rushing to her and putting her shoulder under her arms, helping Lisa reach the sofa.

"Yeah, I am," said Lisa, sprawling on the sofa. "I had a great time."

"Yeah?" Hannah wasn't listening, unable to take her eyes off of Lisa's sweat-covered skin, pink from the alcohol.

"Yeah, and Chet is a great guy!" Lisa yelled, and Hannah covered Lisa's mouth with her hand.

"Shhh, the neighbors will get angry," said Hannah, her eyes sneaking toward the window.

As she moved her hand from Lisa's mouth, she screamed again.

"Fuck them!"

Hannah put her hand on Lisa's lips again. She wasn't smiling anymore, but worry had taken over her.

"What did you drink?" Hannah asked, her eyes set on Lisa's blushing face. "Vodka?"

"Yeah," Lisa smiled, and her head dropped back, her eyes barely staying open.

"You know you can't handle alcohol," Hannah muttered and stood up. "Why did Chet let you drink so much?"

Lisa didn't answer, just shrugged and let her heavy eyelids close. Hannah went into Lisa's bedroom, taking the blanket and bringing it to Lisa. As she spread it over the girl, she stretched the blanket up to her chin and wrapped herself in it. Dozing off in an embryo pose, Lisa took off her hair tie and put the pillow under her head.

Hannah stood with her hands folded, looking down at her friend. Lisa's golden curls were laid out like stems of some magic flower. With her closed, slightly moving eyes and the smiling pouting lips, Lisa resembled a little kid. Her cheeks were flushed, and somehow she looked more beautiful than ever. She was breathing peacefully, and her curved hair fluttered from the gentle air coming out of her nose.

Hannah felt her heart skipping a beat as she realized that soon Chet would take Lisa away from her. She would move in with him and forget all about poor, overweight, introverted Hannah, who once used to be her best friend.

Hannah kneeled before Lisa and softly touched her forehead, tenderly rubbing her fingers against it. Her eyes, locked on the girl, became teary as though she was preparing to say goodbye.

"I'm not asleep," suddenly Lisa whispered and chuckled, her eyes still closed.

Startled and embarrassed, Hannah put her hand down and leaned back. As Lisa opened her eyes, Hannah ran into them, and she felt her face becoming redder than Lisa's. She felt ashamed as though caught in a crime.

"I'm sorry," Lisa's expression got serious, her voice dropped even lower. "I know you're worried about me. I should've at least called you. I'm a bad friend."

A smile rose to Hannah's lips - a kind of smile sister has for her little sibling.

"That's not true," she said. "You are a good friend. Just a little silly, sometimes."

Both of them giggled before exhaustion arrived again, and Lisa put her head down. Hannah stood up, bringing the plastic bucket and putting it under the sofa in case Lisa got sick during the night.

As she heard Lisa's quiet breathing, she turned the lights off and walked to the window. Looking out of it, she examined the people rushing along the busy street. The night had settled into the basins of the city. The yellow streetlights piercing the darkness crept into the room, hitting the furniture and creating elongated shadows on the ceiling. The sound of Lisa's breathing broke the stillness.

"You don't like Chet, do you?" suddenly she asked.

Hannah looked back, seeing Lisa lying with her back at Hannah. She, too, turned around, looking out of the window again.

"Yeah, I don't," she answered honestly.

"Why?" Lisa didn't sound surprised but a bit melancholy.

"I don't know. There's something in him that's hidden. As if he doesn't let anyone fully know him."

Lisa didn't respond. The few seconds of dreadful silence stretched endlessly.

"I just want you to support me," Lisa uttered. "Maybe Chet's not a perfect guy, but he's good. I want you not to worry."

Hannah sighed and set her eyes on the high rises, twinkling in artificial lights. She realized how desperate Lisa sounded as though asking for her consent. Hannah knew that supporting Lisa was the thing a good friend had to do.

"Of course," she muttered. "I'm always going to support you. And this won't be an exception."

"Thank you," Lisa replied quietly.

Hannah inhaled, seeing how the lights started turning off behind the windows. The buildings, like empty boxes of matches, started sinking in dull, thick darkness.

Hannah heard Lisa's deep breathing again. Now she was asleep, finally. Hannah closed the curtains and went to her friend, putting the coverlet over her that Lisa had flopped over. After softly brushing hair off of Lisa's face, Hanna walked into her bedroom and rolled under the blankets, drowning in slumber in a second.

*

With her face dug in the pillow, Lisa heard footsteps and then the curtains being opened. Through her closed eyelids, she saw the light becoming brighter, and she growled, turning her head away from the window. She heard Hannah putting the boiler on and taking a plate out.

As Lisa lay in between being awake and asleep, she tried remembering what had happened the previous night. Still, she couldn't recall a single memory. As she was about to get up, she realized that opening her eyes wasn't as easy as it used to, as if her eyelids were sewn together. Suddenly, she felt a piercing ache through her head as though someone was striking a hammer into her brain. She realized she was hungover.

Turning to her back and clasping both of the hands around her head with inaudible grumbles leaving her lips, Lisa heard Hannah's voice.

"Oh, are you finally awake?"

Lisa recognized tones of frustration through her friend's voice. A few seconds passed before Lisa opened her eyes and sat up on the sofa.

"Yeah," she muttered.

With her messy hair resembling a wild bush, bloodshot

eyes, wide circles under them, and pale skin, Lisa sat on the sofa, trying to grasp the reality.

"What happened?" she asked and put her feet on the floor, realizing she was still in her outfit.

"You came back drunk after midnight," Hannah replied without looking at her, putting butter over a toast. "And fell asleep on the sofa."

"Oh, yeah," Lisa said and remembered her and Chet drinking shots in a bar. She recalled the neon lights in the bar, the colorful tequila glasses, and Chet's glimmering eyes, him driving her home and kissing her before she got out. Lisa remembered Chet's soft lips and his hand around her waist. Somehow, Lisa didn't feel anything thinking of this memory.

What's wrong? Lisa asked herself. *Maybe it didn't happen, and it's just my imagination.*

"How are you feeling?" Hannah's voice interrupted her, and Lisa looked up, seeing Hannah standing with a toast and a cup of tea in her hand. She put them on the table and signaled at Lisa to eat them.

"My head hurts so much," Lisa moaned and stood up, staggering as though her body weighed a ton. Her head got heavier, and the pain - sharper. Each hammer strike was worse than the previous, and Lisa felt like soon, her head would explode and shed into tiny, bloody pieces.

As she sat at the table and bit the toast, Lisa closed her eyes and let out sounds of pleasure.

"You are a lifesaver," she said and looked at Hannah, who sat with her arms folded, looking at Lisa like a worried mother.

"Take some aspirin after you are done eating," she said. "It'll calm down the headache."

Lisa nodded and gulped the tea.

"Don't drink so much another time," said Hannah and stood up. "You were a mess last night."

Lisa swallowed the last bite of the toast and stood up, taking a pill of aspirin out of the cabinet. She peered toward the plastic bucket under the sofa.

"At least I didn't vomit," she snickered, but Hannah didn't laugh, taking the bucket and bringing it back in the bathroom.

"Oh, don't be angry, Hannah," Lisa begged and walked into the bathroom after her, seeing Hannah brushing her teeth.

Lisa leaned on the wall behind her back, looking at Hannah's reflection in the mirror. Hannah cleaned her mouth and began brushing her hair.

"I'm not angry," she said, but her voice told otherwise.

Thinking her friend would forgive her in no time, Lisa looked down at her phone, seeing Chet's message popping up on the screen - just a sentence with heart emojis at the end.

"Oh, Chet's team has a practice today," she said and peeked toward Hannah with sparkling eyes. "Let's go, okay?"

"Are you attending all his practices?" Hannah asked and fell silent before adding. "No, you go. I don't think he wants me there."

"Don't be stupid!" said Lisa and clung to the edge of her shirt like a begging kid. "Please, let's go. It's Saturday anyway; you've got nothing to do."

Hannah looked at her, and Lisa widened her eyes to express her desire as clearly as possible. Then she put her palms together as if about to kneel for prayer. Hannah laughed and shook her head.

"Okay, let's go," she said.

Lisa clapped and turned on the shower.

"I'll be out in a minute," she said and started taking her clothes off even though Hannah was still brushing her hair.

As Lisa flopped the shirt off of her head, she saw Hannah's eyes sneaking toward her and then lowering from embarrassment. Hannah put the brush down and left the room with quick steps. Lisa knew Hannah had often dreamed about having her body, but now her shy look was different from the one adorning Lisa's appearance. It was something else. Hannah's eyes were filled with desire, and it created sexual tension in the room that both - Hannah and Lisa - felt. That's why Hannah rushed out. Because Lisa noticed the passion in her eyes, she caught her in the act.

Lisa's face got red as she stepped out of her pants and stood under the running water. What surprised her the most was that Hannah's stare hadn't made her uncomfortable. On the contrary, it felt much more pleasant than Chet's kiss.

Lisa turned the shower off and stepped out, quickly drying her body while trying to stop thinking about Hanah and her eyes looking at her.

As she stepped out into the living room, Lisa saw Hannah already dressed, sitting on the sofa. The oversized black hoodie covered her body shape, and the thick layers of gothic makeup concealed her skin. Today Hannah's lipstick seemed darker than usual. Somehow, Lisa felt that it was because of Chet as though Hannah knew her style irritated Chet and wanted to provoke him on purpose. Lisa wondered if they would ever be on good terms. Hannah had promised she'd support Lisa, but there was a big difference between supporting her and liking her boyfriend.

Lisa went into her room and threw on a simple sporty shirt and pants, stepping into sneakers and putting her partly wet hair in a ponytail. As she closed the door of her bedroom, she called Hannah.

"Let's go."

Hannah stood up not very enthusiastically, but Lisa sensed that she was forcing herself to show at least traces of eagerness that she didn't really have.

She'll get to like Chet. Eventually. Lisa thought and smiled at Hannah.

"Sorry for being trouble last night," she said after they left the apartment and went outside. "I must've exhausted you."

"It's okay," Hannah smiled, and Lisa sensed how genuine it was. She had often noticed that Hannah built walls while interacting with other people; her movements and manner of talking became a bit staged as if she was trying to fit into people's expectations. But Hannah was always entirely real and honest with Lisa, hundred percent herself.

As they approached the football pitch, Lisa discerned Chet among other players with dark blue uniforms on. They had already started practicing and were drenched in sweat. Under the blazing sunlight, their slippery skin gleamed like the skin of dolphins.

As Chet saw Lisa, he signaled at the players and ran up to her, wrapping his hands around Lisa.

"Ugh, you're sweaty," Lisa chuckled as Chet started kissing her cheeks.

Lisa peered toward Hannah, standing with her hands in the pockets, and silently elbowed Chet, who hadn't even noticed Lisa's friend.

"Oh, hi, Hannah," said Chet with a weak smile and turned to Lisa before Hannah could reply. "Were you okay last night?"

"Yeah, Hannah took care of me," said Lisa, noticing how Chet lost interest as soon as she mentioned Hannah's name.

Meanwhile, Hannah had already taken a seat, looking at the match. As she couldn't hear them anymore, Lisa looked at Chet.

"Did we kiss last night?" she asked quietly.

"Yeah," Chet beamed, and his brows raised from confidence. "You liked it, right?"

"Yeah," Lisa murmured. Hannah would immediately catch tones of hesitation in her voice, but Chet couldn't notice anything.

"Great," he said and kissed her cheek before running and joining the game.

Lisa sat next to Hannah, who didn't move her head; her eyes set on the players, but Lisa knew her mind was flying far away.

Lisa didn't know what to say, and as she was searching for the right words, she saw Chet waving at her with a broad smile. Lisa waved back and clapped.

"Woohoo!" she screamed to encourage Chet even though she knew he didn't need it.

Lisa looked at Hannah, twinkling at her, hoping to receive a smile back. But Hannah sat motionlessly as though immersed in the game. Lisa put her hands down. She fixed her eyes on the players, too, deciding to act just like Hannah and pretend the tension that had been building up between them didn't exist.

CHAPTER 3

The balmy weather foreboded unbearable heat as Hannah sat in the college yard, scrolling through her phone. The fresh leaves rustled on the broad branches above her head as warm breeze slid through them, then lowering and fondling Hannah's ear. She realized she had put her hair up and quickly let it down, pushing it forward over her ears to cover as much of her face as possible.

Despite the sunny day, she wore a long-sleeved black hoodie and jeans in the same color. Hannah seemed out of place between the students with flowery dresses, sleeveless shirts, and short skirts. She looked like a picture cut out from a magazine and glued into a completely different one. Looking around, Hannah realized how much she didn't fit the surroundings, the green scenery, vivid colored clothes, and careless laughter. She would better fit into a cold place, covered with snow, with gloomy sky and grey clouds where no one wants to go outside, where no one cares about other's appearances or style.

Ah, that would be great, Hannah mused. *I'd be perfectly fine in a world where looks don't matter.*

But she knew well that a world like that didn't exist and was just a result of her daydreaming. Sighing, Hannah turned her eyes back on her phone screen, her thumb instinctively sliding up and down on it. As she realized what she was seeing, Hannah's frustration grew deeper, finally turning into anger, and she threw the phone in her bag. Social media was full of girls and their ready-for-summer bodies. The bikinis, hardly covering their tanned skin and fit limbs, made Hannah's insecurities hit the highest level.

She took out her earphones and put them in, trying to shut her brain down and immerse herself in the music. As she was about to close her eyes and doze off, Hannah caught a glimpse of Chet walking out of the college. He walked with a confident smile, his curls bouncing as he walked with wide, steady steps. He looked like a model in a sports advertisement.

Hannah's eyes followed him as he opened his arms, welcomed by a group of boys with a loud cheer. They tapped each other's backs, slightly hugging just like straight boys do when they want to declare they are friends but not more than that. When two girls, with tight dresses hardly covering their thighs, passed by them, the boys threw some remarks.

"Hey, beautiful, why don't you join us?" one of the boys called and spread his hands. The girls smiled, receiving the compliments but passing by without stopping.

Hannah didn't miss how Chet's eyes sneaked toward them, and he rubbed his chin in an ever so vulgar way that shivers of disgust ran down Hannah's spine. He didn't say anything but kept staring at the girls till they disappeared into the building.

Suddenly Chet separated from the group and began walking toward the entrance gates. Looking down at the time, Hannah realized it was still an hour left for Lisa to finish her class, so she decided to follow Chet.

Hannah stood up, walking a few feet behind Chet. As he went out in the streets and hastened his steps, Hannah did the same, trying not to lose him from her sight.

I can't believe I'm spying on him, Hannah thought and chuckled.

She was nervous, but she couldn't fight the feeling that Chet was hiding something. Hannah couldn't let him break Lisa's heart and deceive her. If he was unfaithful, Hannah needed to know to open Lisa's eyes as soon as possible. Her friend didn't believe her, so if Hannah had proof, then perhaps she would.

The streets were busy, and Hannah slid between the people, trying not to push or kick anyone, but it was impossible to walk on the sidewalk without offending people. Heads turned around toward her, faces twisted with anger and frustration.

"Sorry," she kept apologizing while trying not to lose the target from her sight.

While bumping into others, Hannah caught a glimpse of Chet crossing the street.

As she inched her way through the crowd, she looked up, and her heart skipped a beat - she couldn't see Chet anymore.

Fuck I lost him.

Ready to draw in despair, Hannah bent forward, leaning on her knees. Feeling the hot air growing transparent hands, wrapping around her neck and trying to choke her, Hannah started gasping. People kept passing by her with a curious stare, some slowing down and observing her, hesitating to ask if she was okay.

The surroundings began spinning, and Hannah felt like soon she'd lose consciousness and sprawl in the middle of the street. Suddenly, someone touched her shoulder.

"Hannah?"

She looked up, seeing Lisa looking down with a concerned face.

"What's wrong?" she asked and helped her straighten her back. "Are you okay?"

Again, Lisa turned out to be the only one helping her, the only one touching her and asking what she needed to be asked the most.

Sitting on the bench, Hannah exhaled. Her pulse turned back to normal, and her skin stopped sweating.

"No, I'm not okay," said Hannah and pulled the hoodie off of her. "I can't take this heat anymore."

She saw stares toward her round, bare arms. Hannah shrugged from discomfort and looked at Lisa.

"Yeah, give me that!" said Lisa and seized the hoodie from Hannah's hands, shoving it down her bag. "You don't need this now. No one can take this heat, and you want to do it in winter's clothing?"

Hannah gulped from the bottle of water and closed her eyes for a second before Lisa's voice made them open widely.

"What are you doing here?"

Unable to come up with an excuse, Hannah looked down and tried to shoot back the question.

"What are you doing here? Don't you have a class?"

This question seemed to embarrass Lisa as she put her hair behind her ear - a habit when she was nervous or ashamed.

"I skipped it," she said and twinkled at Hannah. She realized Lisa was begging for understanding. "I'm going to see Chet. He asked me. Skipping one class is no big deal, right?"

Hannah fell silent. This wasn't usual for Lisa as she rarely skipped a class, only when she was sick. And even when Hannah dreaded getting up and tried to come up with thousand reasons to avoid attending a class, Lisa was the one dragging her out of bed and convincing Hannah to go. Lisa would say that listening to a professor was the foundation for their education.

Looking at Lisa, Hannah thought she was looking at someone else rather than at her childhood friend. She wondered how Chet - a pretty boy with no personality - could change her so much, rob Lisa of her most precious traits that Hannah loved so much.

Lisa kept staring for a while, and Hannah couldn't scold her, feeling like she'd start crying.

"Yeah, it's no big deal," said Hannah, what Lisa wanted to hear.

A smile of relief rose to Lisa's lips, and she leaned in, clasping her arms around Hannah.

"Thanks," she whispered in her ear, and Hannah felt goosebumps running down her skin. There was something so tense about Lisa's voice and her lips being so close to Hannah's skin.

Lisa leaned back and stood up, fixing her hair and looking into her phone screen, using it as a mirror. Her eyes observed her reflection as though trying to find a tiny blemish or an untamed hair strand. Lisa had never been obsessed with her looks, and even when preparing for an important day, she'd only glance at the mirror. Hannah got confused, looking at Lisa, who seemed to be transforming into any other ordinary girl.

"How do I look?" Lisa asked and glided her hands down her waist.

That's when Hannah realized that she wore a dress - nothing extra, but a thin white dress, reaching her knees, covering her shoulders, unbuttoned to let the cleavage peek through a little. The spotless fabric had enveloped around Lisa's body, adorning her. She looked beautiful but not unique - like a birthday gift wrapped in flashy paper.

"Since when do you wear dresses?" Hannah couldn't contain the shock anymore.

Not expecting this reaction, Lisa looked down as though trying to see what was wrong with her outfit.

"I don't know, I wanted to try something new," she uttered and bent her lips in dissatisfaction.

Hannah couldn't take her eyes off her friend, who looked like a dressed-up puppy being shown off by her owner. The owner, in this case, was Chet, who'd show Lisa off to his friends. Hannah knew Lisa tried to change because of Chet, and he had successfully managed to turn her into a mediocre girl with nice hair, pretty eyes but nothing else to offer. Like her quirky traits and habits, Lisa's style had begun to slowly disappear too, and alter, becoming something depleted of individuality.

Hannah pursed her lips to stop all the words rushing to her mouth. If she let them escape, she knew they would reveal her hatred toward Chet. She inhaled, trying to control her emotions, and stared up at Lisa. She looked beautiful, undoubtedly. So, Hannah decided to concentrate on the good and throw the bad to the back of her mind.

"The dress really suits you," she said to Lisa, whose sad expression immediately got replaced by delight.

"Thanks!" she exclaimed. "I'm going to go, now, then. I'll see you later."

Lisa waved and turned around, crossing the street just like Chet had done earlier as though following his footsteps. Hannah watched her back and the edges of white dress fluttering around her knees, neatly brushed hair falling to her shoulders.

Anyone would fall for her, Hannah thought and wondered that maybe Chet loved Lisa too, in a different way, not as deeply as Hannah did, but perhaps she doubted Chet too much.

Hannah watched Lisa till she walked down the street and disappeared in the corner. Now she had to bear few hours without her. Sighing, Hannah stood up, instinctively shoving her hands into her pockets when she realized that Lisa had taken her hoodie with her. Embarrassed by the sudden awareness that her bare arms were uncovered, Hannah hastened her steps toward home.

*

The familiar traffic noise rang into Hannah's ears as she and Lisa walked out in the streets the following day, headed toward the college. The traffic lights twinkled in vivid colors as the cars rolled by with hip-hop music flowing out of their open windows. It was summer, and even though people still needed to work or study, they tried to feel the warmth and at least pretend that life got better.

Hannah and Lisa walked silently next to each other. Being so quiet in one another's company was unusual, and Hannah couldn't fight the feeling that something was wrong. She peeked toward Lisa, whose reflective face revealed that the girl was sinking deep into her thoughts. Hannah wanted to know what she was thinking about but couldn't dare to ask, feeling like she'd step over the boundaries.

Lisa wore her usual outfit - jeans and shirt, but she had put a little more makeup on - red lipstick and mascara and had put her hair down, letting the golden curls shine under the sunlight. Hannah realized she'd prepared to meet Chet.

"How was your date yesterday?" Hannah asked to break the silence.

"Good," Lisa smiled weakly. "There's a new cafe down the street. We should go there together."

Hannah nodded and was about to reply when Chet appeared out of thin air, rushing to Lisa and lifting her. They had reached the college yard gates, and the students kept gawking at the couple. Lisa clung to him, wrapping her arms around his shoulders and lightly kissing his lips as Chet stretched his neck.

Instinctively, Hannah turned her head around, looking down at her feet. She had never seen Lisa kiss someone, and only catching a glimpse of it was enough for the image to stick in her mind. Hannah wondered how nice it must've felt to touch Lisa's soft lips, and the jealousy grew deeper in her, envy that she wasn't Chet.

As Chet put Lisa down, he put his arm around her shoulder.

"Let's go to the movies," he said. "There's a new action thriller out."

"But I have a class," Lisa answered.

"Skip it," Chet said, which sounded more like a demand than a suggestion. Then he looked at Hannah. "I'm sure Hannah can cover for you."

Hannah clenched her jaws, ready to protest, but as she ran into Lisa's eyes, she held back.

"Yeah, you can, right, Hannah?" Lisa asked. Lisa didn't seem excited but like a confused child obeying adults' orders.

"How?" Hannah asked, still feeling Chet's glare.

"Think of some excuse," said Chet and turned around, holding Lisa's hand. "Let's go."

Lisa glanced back before Chet pulled her closer, and they blended into the crowd.

Sighing, Hannah turned around, walking into the yard. As she walked, she felt like she was missing something. She was so uncomfortable, as if she was naked. She hastened her steps, almost running into the building.

Heading toward the classroom, Lisa's face kept floating to the surface of Hannah's mind. She remembered her eyes and the confusion infused with disappointment forming in them as Chet had suggested skipping the class. Hannah knew her friend didn't want it, but in front of Chet, as though she lost her power, Lisa became weak, obedient, vulnerable. He was strong, tall, and powerful, looking down on Lisa, and Hannah felt like even his physical appearance intimidated her friend.

Or maybe she's trying to make Chet like her more, Hannah thought.

Either way, Hannah didn't like the changes Lisa was going through. She didn't like the new version of her friend and wished for old Lisa that she knew so well.

While sinking into the thoughts, Lisa stepped into the classroom through the open door and took her seat, glancing toward her right where Lisa should've been sitting. Hannah looked around, seeing that everyone sat in couples, chatting cheerfully, carelessly, laughing, and joking. Their beaming faces, depleted of any worry, looked like faces of soulless toys displayed for window shopping.

The sound of heels clanking on the floor halted the noise, and the students sitting on the tables jumped down, quickly settling into their seats. Others straightened their backs and neatly put hands in front of them like first-graders.

The professor walked inside, standing in front of the class, and glided her hands on her slicked-back hair, her eyes skimming across the room.

"Good morning," she said with a monotonous voice as though radio talked instead of a person.

"Good morning, Mrs. Ambrose," the students replied simultaneously.

The teacher put on her glasses that kept sliding down her nose, reading out names from the journal. As she read Lisa and looked up to search for her with her eyes, Hannah cleared her throat, drawing attention.

"Lisa is very sick," she said.

"Oh, what's wrong?" Mrs. Ambrose sounded concerned, and she creased her brows. She loved Lisa as Lisa was one of the best students. Hannah felt guilty for lying to her, sensing that the teacher would truly be worried.

"She's got a fever," Hannah muttered. "The doctor said she'd be fine soon."

"Good," Mrs. Ambrose smiled and continued reading the names.

Hannah exhaled from relief and looked out of the window, her eyes sadly running across the street, imagining what Lisa and Chet were doing: sitting in the dark, only them in the empty rows of chairs, the huge screen brightening their faces, the loud voices blaring in the auditorium. Hannah's mind slipped to the visions she didn't want to see: Chet Kissing Lisa and sliding his hand under her shirt, Lisa winding her arms around his neck and opening her mouth wider, their tongues entangling and lips getting swollen.

Hannah squeezed her eyes shut, trying to erase the image from her head.

"Hannah!" suddenly she heard the teacher's voice and looked up, seeing Mrs. Abrose standing at the blackboard, writing a new formula. "Concentrate!"

"Sorry," Hannah muttered and heard few giggles thrown at her. She shrugged, hiding her neck in her shoulders and watching the teacher as she pressed the chalk against the board, making a screeching sound. Hannah pinned her eyes on it, but she couldn't see the formula or the teacher. All she saw was Lisa and Chet kissing, and her face reddened from fury.

After an hour, as Hannah walked out of the class, she landed her eyes in Lisa and Chet walking toward her. They seemed cheerful, twinkling at each other, and Hannah couldn't help herself but think that the image she'd created in her mind had come to reality.

Lisa gave a little wave as they saw Hannah, but Chet's expression loosened, his smile melted, and he gripped Lisa's waist tighter.

"Gotta go," said Lisa and gave him a pack, leaning back as Chet tried to kiss her more. Disappointed, Chet let her go, and after throwing a quick glare toward Hannah, he turned around, walking down the hallway.

"How was the class? Did Mrs. Ambrose ask for me? " Lisa asked and licked her lips as though trying to remove Chet's taste.

Hannah's eyes froze on them for a moment, thinking they seemed fuller and redder than usual.

Swelled, the thought lanced her mind. *Did they even watch the movie?*

Trying to snap herself out of it, Hannah smiled sheepishly and Looked into her eyes.

"Yeah, she did, and I said you're sick," she replied.

"Thank you," Lisa let out with tones of shame in her voice. "I'll never do it again."

Looking at her, Hannah thought that Lisa was genuine but only momentarily. As soon as Chet would suggest a new idea, she'd follow him along without much consideration.

Lisa glided her tongue over her lips again and pinned her eyes on the floor. Hannah sensed the transparent wall that had been building up between them, raising again.

"You don't have a class now, right?" Lisa asked.

"No, I have a break till 12," Hannah responded, checking the time.

Nodding, Lisa turned toward the stairs. "I'll see you at home then. Don't wait for me."

Hannah opened her mouth to protest but closed it immediately, realizing Lisa had planned to meet Chet after the classes too.

"Okay," she muttered, and without giving Lisa another look, Hannah turned back, walking out of the college.

Trying to control the doubts that kept filling her up, Hannah noticed that her shoelaces were loose. She kneeled, bending to tie them as she felt a kick from behind. Standing on only one leg, Hannah couldn't keep the balance and was thrown forward, leaning against the ground with her elbows. She heard quiet giggles and snickers from the back and saw two girls passing by, seemingly the ones who had kicked her.

Hannah stood up, rubbing her knees and elbows to remove the dirt, still listening to the whispers and mocking sounds forming around her. As she looked up, she saw Chet with his friend group, suppressing his laughter while looking at her.

Hannah felt anger boiling blood inside her as it rushed to her head, making it ache from pain. But the more she stared, the more she realized that it's who Chet was - another bully.

Hannah walked to one of the chairs to catch a breath and calm herself down as she noticed Chet walking out in the streets.

Now it was the perfect time to spy on him as Lisa was in her class and Hannah had nothing to do. Without hesitation, she stood up, following Chet's steps.

As he walked outside with hands in the pockets and open shoulders, Hannah scurried after him, hiding behind people as Chet would look back from time to time. This habit of him being suspicious about his surroundings doubted Hannah even more.

What is he looking out for? She thought, not moving her eyes off of him.

Chet crossed the street, and Hannah did the same, falling back with a few feet, but she stopped on the sidewalk as she saw Chet turning into an alley.

Hannah frowned, watching the boy disappear into the dark path between two buildings. Wondering what he might be doing there, Hannah decided it wasn't time to chicken out and followed him with quick steps.

The doubt that Chet was cheating on Lisa grew more and more prominent, getting better of Hannah. The dark and secluded alley proved her suspicions.

She walked into the alley, seeing Chet's white shirt shining in the gloom. Hannah hid behind the trash bin, peeking from behind it and watching Chet as he stopped and looked to his right and then left, seemingly waiting for someone.

Suddenly a voice reached Hannah's ear, and she distinguished a silhouette approaching Chet as he turned toward it and spread his arms.

Hannah's heart started pounding, thinking she had caught Chet in the act. But in a second, her agitation vanished. Squinting her eyes, she saw that the outline was of a boy, and they didn't even touch each other, standing in the distance.

Disappointed, Hannah kept on observing, and soon her

curiosity bobbed up again. Chet skimmed over the surroundings and took something out of his pocket. The green paper rustled as he put it into the boy's hand.

Money! Hannah hardly contained a gasp. *What is he buying?*

The boy, wearing ratty jeans and an oversized sweater, soon threw a little package that fell into Chet's arms. Chet nodded, and the boy turned around, fading into the dark.

Hannah stretched her neck, narrowing her eyes, almost falling out of her hiding place to see what Chet was holding. In a minute, she tutted and bit her lip from frustration.

"Fuck!" she whispered. "It's just a cigarette!"

Chet took one out, tucking it in the corner of his mouth and liting it up. He sucked it in so hard that his chest expanded. With a pleased face as though he was sinking in ecstasy, Chet let the smoke out that piled up in a cloud above his head, slowly dispersing.

Hannah knew why Chet acted like smoking was a crime. If his coach heard about it, he'd have problems. Chet was the lead football player, a sportsman. And smoking for athletes was equal to taking drugs. The smoke filling up their lungs wasn't less than a crime. They followed strict diet rules, training every day and controlling the calories, even the amount of water they took.

Hannah leaned against the wall, exhaling from disappointment. As she comprehended her feelings, she felt the urge to slap herself in the face.

Why am I sad that my doubts turned out to be false? She asked herself. *I should be happy for Lisa.*

But even though her mind and logic told her so, her heart said otherwise. Chet was perfect, and even her little hope that he had a flaw had died. Now Chet had officially won against her. She lost. Lisa would never leave him, and they'd live happily ever after, just like in fairy tales.

Sighing, Hannah glanced at Chet again, who kept on smoking, the cigarette quickly shortening in his fingers. His eyes following the smoke looked so sad that Hannah pitied him for a moment - he had to be so careful and hide for something so meaningless.

Suddenly, Chet's phone rang, and he answered it, the smile spreading on his face.

"Babe! Is the class over?" he asked and flicked the cigarette butt, crushing it with his heel. "I'm gonna be right there."

Realizing he was talking to Lisa, Hannah turned around, hurriedly leaving the alley. She rubbed her eyes, trying not to let the welling up tears escape.

I'm a total failure, she thought before crossing the street, working her way between the tight crowd.

*

The sun had suddenly hidden behind the gray clouds that had crashed into each other, spreading above the city. The clear blue sky got covered with clouds heavy with water, and soon the lightning split them in half, brightening the surroundings with dreadful silver, followed by the thunder.

The earsplitting sound woke Hannah up from her nap, and startled, she jumped up from the bed. Looking out, she saw the darkened surroundings and the sky getting ready to soak the city. Everyone had escaped into the comfort of their homes and shut the windows. Hannah skimmed the street, looking for Lisa.

As she looked down at her phone, a message appeared.

"I'll be home in 5 minutes," Lisa was texting.

Hannah looked up at the sky, worried that Lisa had to walk all the way. In a minute, raindrops fell on the ground that soon turned into heavy rain. The drops dribbled down the windows, hitting the glass. The trees swayed under the heavy beads as they kept bathing the surroundings.

Suddenly, Hannah noticed a car rolling by and pulling up across the building. The door opened, and Lisa jumped out, running toward the house.

"Chet drove her," Hannah mumbled to herself and didn't know if she was jealous or happy that Lisa didn't have to walk.

But before Lisa could cross the street, she already got

drenched within seconds. So, as she opened the door and stepped inside, the water dropped everyone around her in the apartment.

"God, what the hell happened to the weather?" Lisa exclaimed and laughed, shutting the door behind. "It's so dark in here," she hit the light switch.

Leaving traces of wet shoes, Lisa walked inside and slipped off her sneakers.

"I'll get you a towel," said Hannah and rushed into the bathroom, bringing the towel.

"Thanks," Lisa said and grabbed it, beginning to dry her hair.

Hannah stood, watching her without realizing it. The wet shirt clung onto Lisa's torso, and the black bra was visible through it. The jeans had stuck around her legs like a fossil, making it obvious how uncomfortable they were. The water dripped from Lisa's hair, crawling down her neck and sneaking into her chest.

Looking up, Lisa's eyes ran into Hannah's, and she realized she'd been staring. Hannah turned her head around, but it was already late; Lisa had noticed her look. Embarrassment spreading into her, Hannah wanted to run away and hide somewhere far, hide from her shame.

"Ah, these pants are killing me," said Lisa and unbuttoned them.

Hannah swallowed and turned her back at her, looking out of the window only to realize that it reflected Lisa. For a second, Hannah thought of going into her room, but her eyes were glued on Lisa's reflection. She couldn't move.

Lisa unbuttoned the pants and pulled them down, finally slipping out of them. Her white underwear was wet, clasping to her skin. Unconsciously, Hannah bit her lip as something got stuck in her throat.

Why is she doing this? The thought pierced her mind. She can do it in her room, can't she?

Hannah wondered if Lisa was doing this on purpose to see Hannah's reaction or even to provoke her. Since the bathroom accident - when Hannah's eyes sneaked toward Lisa as she was taking off her clothes - Hannah felt some tension building up between them. Part of it was because of Chet, but the other part wasn't jealousy or doubts - it was a passion that both Lisa and Hannah sensed. As though turning into a bubble, the agitation swallowed the girls, distancing them from the outer world and leaving them with only one another.

Hannah turned around, looking at Lisa as she stood, holding onto her pants. Suddenly, as if she realized she wasn't alone, Lisa looked down at herself, and her cheeks blushed. She chuckled nervously.

"I'm gonna..." her voice broke. "I'm gonna go change."

Lisa hurried into her room and closed it. Exhaling, Hannah flopped on the couch, digging her face in her hands.

"What the hell was that?" she asked herself.

Hannah leaned back and stared at the ceiling for a moment, trying to grasp the reality, wondering what Lisa's blushing and embarrassed expression were about.

In a few minutes, the door opened, and Lisa came out, now with dry clothes on, but her hair was still damp, laying on her shoulders.

"Want some coffee?" she asked and scratched her head.

Hannah nodded, and Lisa went to the coffee machine, turning it on. As she stood with her back at her, Hannah realized Lisa tried avoiding looking at her. She was still embarrassed. They had seen each other in underwear many times, but this one was different. It hadn't been innocent or friendly but had reeked of sexual tension.

Lisa handed Hannah one cup and sat next to her, silently sipping hers.

"I want to ask you something," she said suddenly and looked at Hannah.

"What is it?" Hannah asked and put the cup down.

Lisa hesitated and pursed her lips to one side.

"Come on, what's up?" Hannah scoffed.

"I need money," Lisa smiled awkwardly. "For the date with Chet."

Hannah didn't expect this and fell silent for a second.

"Doesn't he pay for dates?" she finally asked.

"He does, and that's why I want to pay this time or at least split the bill with him," Lisa started explaining herself. "I feel embarrassed. He's the one always paying."

"If he's inviting you, why do you feel guilty for not paying?" Hannah asked, getting irritated.

"It's not only his date, is it?" Lisa locked eyes with her. "It's mine too. I want to pay too."

Hannah wanted to say that Chet was rich and he didn't mind spending money on dates, but she changed her mind. She didn't want to hurt Lisa's feelings as she saw her friend was already ashamed enough.

"Okay," Hannah said and stood up, bringing her wallet and handing Lisa two hundred dollars of cash. "Here, take it."

Lisa took the money, at first watching it with confusion as if she couldn't believe what she was holding. Finally, she jumped up and hugged Hannah.

"Thank you!" she exclaimed. "I will pay you back. I promise."

"I know," Hannah tapped on her back, feeling Lisa's chest against hers.

"I love you," said Lisa.

"I love you too," Hannah replied.

As she listened to the raindrops softly tapping on the window, Hannah realized that there were more than friendly sentiments in Lisa's "I love you."

*

The chalk being dragged across the board snapped Lisa out of her afternoon nap. She opened her eyes, blankly looking into space. She realized she was in the class and quietly growled, putting her head back on the desk. Somehow exhaustion had settled into her bones, making her sleepy during the day. The basketball practices had taken their toll, and on top of that, Chet had been demanding meeting up too often.

The students began standing up and leaving the room with loud chatter. Lisa, too, pulled herself up from the chair and walked outside. As she landed her eyes on Hannah sitting with an open book on her lap, a smile began shaping on Lisa's mouth. Seeing her friend always made warmth pour into her. She'd become happy just like some people do by watching cute puppies. Looking at Hannah was enough for Lisa to forget all her worries and become the funny and quirky girl that Hannah loved so much.

"Oh, Lisa!" Hannah caught her staring and waved. Lisa knew Hannah felt the same way as she'd noticed that Hannah would begin beaming like the sun while being around Lisa. They both made each other happy. What else could Lisa ask for?

"Hey, what are you doing?" she asked and flopped next to her.

"Oh, I'm reading about this flower," Hannah replied with enlarged eyes and pointed at the picture in the book. "Look how beautiful it is! As if it's from another planet, somewhere very far away."

Following her stare, Lisa saw a photo of a red flower with gleaming, phosphoric lines across its stems.

"It really is stunning," she responded and looked at Hannah, who still gazed at the image with kid's curiosity. Little stars twinkled in her eyes, and Lisa couldn't help but think that Hannah herself was as beautiful as the flower.

Something about Hannah was very alluring. Maybe it was her undying interest in unique things or the way her face would lit up while talking about them, but Lisa felt that she was unconsciously fighting the urge to kiss her.

Lisa kept watching as Hannah couldn't even notice, still keeping on about the flower. Her black hair that had grown a little fluttered in the slight wind, and the light hitting her forehead formed mysterious shadows on her face, her long lashes touching her cheeks while lowering and her lips pouting, taking a color and a shape of a ripe peach.

As Hannah's voice started getting muffled in the background and her face getting sharper, Lisa felt her throat getting dry and sweat coming out of every pore of her skin. She had never felt this way before, and she swallowed, leaning back as she realized she could smell Hannah's scent - the soft odor of fresh laundry and apple juice that Hannah had drunk that morning. Lisa felt like Hannah was seducing her but without being aware. And it made everything even worse.

How can I be tempted by my best friend? The thought arrived. *She isn't even flirting. Am I crazy?!*

"Lisa, are you okay?" Hannah's voice threw her back to reality. "You look like you're dozing off."

"Yeah, I'm a bit tired," Lisa chuckled nervously.

"You've been practicing a lot lately," Hannah mentioned with a worried face. "You should take a rest."

"You're right," Lisa nodded with a smile. Watching into Hannah's eyes, she hardly stopped herself from caressing her cheek. "Wanna go to the park and eat some ice cream?"

"Yeah," Hannah stood up, offering a hand. "Let's go."

Lisa took her hand, and they went through the open gates. As she walked beside her, looking at her profile and serene expression, Lisa thought she could walk miles and go everywhere as long as she held Hannah's hand.

After buying ice cream, they went into the nearby park, where they spent a lot of time after classes. Or at least, they used to before Chet appeared in Lisa's life.

Sitting on the bench, Lisa looked at the kids on the playground. Their high-pitched, careless laughter filled the place, even overshadowing the singing of the birds. The parents watched from a distance while chatting with one another. The sound of cars rolling by was muffled, and Lisa felt like they had traveled to a resort, far from the busy city.

"Let's go somewhere when the holiday starts," she suggested and licked the ice cream. "To a beach or something. What do you think?"

Hannah smiled and shrugged.

"Anywhere will be fun as long as we're together," she responded.

Lisa smiled at her, feeling how genuine her words were.

"You're right," she said. "I'm never bored with you."

"Same here," Hannah giggled. "That's why we stuck so long, I think. Friendships rarely last for years."

Lisa nodded and widened her smile, now stretching from ear to ear.

She noticed how reluctant Hannah was about eating the ice cream. She slowly ate it and would quickly put her head up if someone passed by them. So, the ice cream melted and dribbled down her hand.

"Oh, fuck," Hannah cussed and looked at her chest where the melted cream had dropped, staining the shirt.

"Here, don't worry," Lisa said and pulled wipes out of her bag. She leaned in, rubbing the stain off of her chest. Suddenly, she looked up, running into Hannah's eyes, realizing she was touching right where her breast was.

"Oh, sorry," she exclaimed and pulled herself backward, blushing and looking away. She felt how her face begun burning.

"It's okay," she heard Hannah's voice and a chuckle. Despite the attempt, Lisa still noticed embarrassment and nervousness in her voice.

An awkward silence ensued for a few seconds before Lisa gained her courage and looked back at her. Hannah sat quietly and had thrown away the ice cream.

"You should've eaten it," said Lisa, making Hannah giggle.

"I couldn't, but my shirt ate it."

They both laughed, and Lisa felt the ice melting. She wondered how Hannah always managed to ease an awkward situation. She had real talent.

Suddenly Hannah fell silent and started twiddling with the thread coming undone from her pants. Lisa sensed that she was preparing to say something, and it would take Hannah a while to finally let the words out. Lisa knew that she always took her time, searching for the right words, never letting herself blab or slip anything that'd come to her mind but sometimes it got too time-consuming. A stranger wouldn't be able to bear the silence, but Lisa was used to it, now patiently waiting for Hannah to start talking.

"Can I ask you something?" Hannah finally spoke and glanced at her, quickly looking back at the playground as though embarrassed by her question.

"Yeah," Lisa chuckled and swallowed the last bite of her ice cream. "What is it?"

As Hannah turned her head, Lisa saw her flushed cheeks, red like a radish.

"Are you and Chet..." Hannah started, and her voice broke that confused her even more. "Are you and Chet doing it? You know. Sex."

Not expecting this question, Lisa widened her eyes and coughed, then nervously chuckled.

"No, of course," she replied. "It's not that serious."

She remembered the day at the movies and Chet's hand sliding across her shoulders, then down her waist. She recalled his lips, eager to kiss hers and his strong body trying to wrap around Lisa. Lisa also remembered how unpleasant the feeling was and how she could smell Chet's excitement, how she had leaned back and shaken her head.

"You don't want it?" Chet had asked as if surprised Lisa didn't feel the same way he did.

"No, Chet, I don't think I'm ready," Lisa had replied but without any shame. All she had wanted was to leave.

"It's okay. I'll wait until you are ready," Chet had smiled and put his head back, trying to contain the enthusiasm that had been bursting out of him a minute ago. Lisa had smiled quietly, holding back from saying that she would never be ready to take this step with him.

Now, as she stared across her as if seeking to distinguish something out of thin air, Lisa realized that those feelings she had felt with Chet would never fade until she'd find someone she really loved. Chet wasn't the one, and she had accepted it. She didn't love him, and she wasn't sure if she even liked him.

Then why am I with him? She asked herself.

Maybe it was because everyone around her had a partner or that she felt some pressure from the world to be like others. But the truth was - she didn't know Chet, the pretty boy who seemed too self-absorbed to notice her emotions. And she didn't love him at all, not even a bit. That's why every touch, every kiss had felt so cold as though her blood froze while being with Chet.

Lisa had heard that when being around someone who attracts you, you feel yourself becoming weightless like a feather, your heart starts pounding, and all you want to do is to touch and kiss that person. While being around them, you two are the only people in the whole world, and nothing else matters.

Lisa didn't feel like this around Chet. But she knew when she felt all these emotions - while being with Hannah.

Breathing in, Lisa looked at her friend, who seemed relieved by her answer. Hannah couldn't hide the satisfaction and the smile curving her lips.

"I thought you and Chet were getting serious," she said, attempting to sound concerned but failed.

Lisa, drowning in her thoughts, stared at her, feeling her pulse increasing.

"Lisa?" Hannah waved in front of her eyes. "You okay?"

Realizing she'd ignored her words, Lisa shook her head.

"Yeah, I'm okay," she said and swallowed. But she wasn't okay. Something strange happened inside her, in her heart and mind. A realization was slowly arriving.

"I said that it seemed like you two were serious," Hannah repeated, now puzzled by Lisa's odd behavior. "You spend so much time together."

"Yeah, but we are just going around in cafes and movies," Lisa responded, trying to control her voice that somehow seemed to get hoarse. "We don't really talk about anything."

"Then what do you do?" Hannah asked.

"Nothing in particular," Lisa said and got thinking. "Now, as I'm thinking of it, we spend time so aimlessly. It's even boring."

The kids stopped playing as their mothers held their hands,

heading home. The sun had passed the zenith, and the orange light slowly faded; the birds halted singing too, preparing their nests for a good night's sleep. A cool zephyr made the trees sway and quickly slid above Lisa's skin. She trembled as goosebumps covered her arms.

"Here, put this on," said Hannah, taking her jacket out of her bag, winding it around Lisa's shoulders.

"Thanks," Lisa said, slipping her hands in the sleeves.

"Wanna go home?" Hannah asked, her eyes searching her face.

Lisa locked her eyes on her. The sun was slowly sinking behind the horizon, and the deep yellow light hit Hannah's face, giving it an ethereal shine. A sweet smile danced on her lips, and Lisa felt the longing to feel them.

"No, I want to be here for a while with you," said Lisa.

"Me too," Hannah replied.

As she looked at the sunset, Lisa felt Hannah's hand squeezing hers. Suddenly the realization that had been hiding in the back of her head found its way into her mind, making her heart skip a beat. Lisa looked at Hannah, pursing her lips to contain the thoughts - Hannah was the one she loved.

CHAPTER 4

The teacher's monotonous voice kept filling the room as the students got more and more disinterested. The teacher, ignoring the chatter almost overshadowing her speech, continued talking while sitting behind her wooden desk, occasionally glancing at the book spread in front of her.

The students had already given in the enthusiasm of the summer holidays approaching and had turned toward each other, blabbering and laughing without considering the time and place. As though the professor didn't even exist, they had turned their back at her, chattering about their plans, some showing each other photos of swimwear, some choosing a place for spending the vacation.

Hannah, the only one still listening to the teacher, had rested her face on her palm, looking at the woman who herself seemed bored of the class. Suddenly Hannah felt tingling on her arm and looked to her right, seeing Lisa leaning in with a playful smile. Hannah smiled too, sensing that Lisa was about to suggest something rebellious as she always did.

"Let's get out of here," she whispered, and her eyes sneaked toward the professor.

"What?" Hannah giggled from surprise, following Lisa's stare and seeing the professor almost dozing off while still talking. She looked like a sleepwalker. She had put her head down as though reading from the book, but her eyelids were trying to stay open as her lips kept moving almost instinctively. Hannah knew the professor wanted nothing but to go home, far away from the brats surrounding her. She sometimes forgot that teachers were humans, too, but in times like this, she'd get reminded that they were no different from the others.

"Yeah, look at her," Lisa cunningly bit her lower lip. "She won't notice a thing."

Hannah shook her head and peeped toward the slightly open door.

"Come on; twenty minutes are still left," Lisa insisted. "You wanna be here when we can be outside? Look how nice the weather is. And the professor has already explained the new lesson."

Looking out of the window, Hannah saw the sunshine bathing the place in warmth, the light glistening on the blossoming flowers and green bushes. The birds flying under the clear sky and even butterflies had appeared, fluttering their thin, colorful wings.

She felt the urge to obey Lisa and break the rule for the first time. She had always tried to behave according to what others said, but now, adorning the outside world and feeling Lisa's eagerness, she could fight the desire anymore.

I deserve to fuck up a little, she thought and beamed at Lisa.

"Okay, let's go," she said and grabbed her bag.

They stood up, silently walking toward the door on tiptoes. The students, immersed in their conversations, didn't even notice as Lisa and Hannah slipped through the door. Hannah glanced back at the professor one last time, but she sat in the same pose, still talking more to herself than to the class.

Hannah ran next to Lisa with quiet laughter, holding her hand, feeling like a bird escaping from a cage. They rushed into the hallway and then out of the building. The yard was vacant as everyone else was still in class.

"Ah, that felt good, didn't it?" Lisa asked, her smile as bright as the sun.

"Yeah, it felt damn good!" Hannah laughed. "We should do this often."

"Oh, look at you," Lisa widened her eyes. "A nice girl turning rebellious?"

"Why not?" Hannah winked, making her friend laugh out

loud.

As they took a breath, Lisa put her arm around Hannah's shoulder.

"It's been a while since we spent the whole day together," said Lisa and lowered her eyes, realizing that it was her fault as she'd been going out with Chet. "Why don't we catch up today?"

"What do you want to do?" Hannah asked, willing to go with whatever Lisa would decide.

"What about a pool?" Lisa's eyes started sparkling. "It's so hot today. It will be nice!"

Hannah's smile vanished, and she looked down at her feet. She hadn't worn a swimsuit in years since she had realized how people looked at her in pools. Hannah used to have fun in swimming pools as she loved water when she was a kid, but as time went on and she became aware of her weight and people's attitude toward it, she had given up on enjoying swimming in public places.

"Oh, come on, Hannah," Lisa let out, sensing Hannah's hesitation. "Just fuck everyone else and imagine it's just you and me. Let's have some fun. You and me. I miss it."

Hannah looked at Lisa and her blue eyes, clear like the sky, begging for consent. It was true - they hadn't had fun in a while, and Hannah missed it too. Staring at Lisa's childish features, Hannah realized she couldn't reject her.

"Okay, let's go!" said Hannah. How long would she be hiding in a shadow because of others? Hannah was tired of constantly thinking about her appearance. And now, all she wanted was to enjoy her day with Lisa.

"You are the best!" Lisa exclaimed and hugged her. "Come on, let's buy swimsuits and go."

The store was right across the street, and they went inside, starting to walk down the aisles of clothes. The people were choosing outfits, and the flashy garments filled the shelves.

"Let's just grab whatever and go," Lis suggested. "We should be there before the sun goes down."

Hannah nodded, even a bit relieved she wouldn't have to

try on the swimsuits. She knew seeing herself in the mirror would make her change her mind about going.

Suddenly a consultant appeared with a formal smile, blocking their way.

"What are you looking for?" she asked, looking at Lisa.

"Swimsuits," she replied. "For my friend and me."

"Oh," the consultant's smile thinned as she skimmed Hannah from head to toe. Hannah felt her eyes judging and shrugged. "I'll be back in a minute," she said and scurried away.

Lisa smiled at Hannah as they waited before the girl appeared with two swimsuits. She shoved the red one into Lisa's hands.

"This is S size; it will fit you perfectly," she said with a broad smile before turning to Hannah. "This black is XL. We don't have a bigger size."

Two emotions started fighting inside Hannah: anger and shame, but suddenly, Lisa's eyes friskily sneaked toward her, and she shoved the black swimwear into the girl's hands.

"She doesn't need a bigger size," Lisa emitted and widened her eyes as though waiting for her to get moving. The bossy vibes made Hannah chuckle. "And black?!" Lisa gasped and clenched her chest as if she'd been stabbed. "Who needs black in summer?! Find something colorful for my friend. Yello, orange, red. Whatever!"

The girl blushed and quickly turned around, vanishing with the black bikini. Rising her brows in pride, Lisa bobbed her shoulders.

"You almost made her cry," Hannah whispered and cuffed her arm.

"I could've threatened her that I'd tell her boss what a shitty consultant she is," said Lisa and flipped her hair, looking around as though she'd done someone a favor. "But I didn't. I'm basically an angel."

Hannah laughed out loud, forgetting the time and place for a moment. Heads turned around, and she covered her mouth. "Sorry."

The girl came back with a yellow swimsuit and a broad

smile, showing the bikini to Hannah.

"Thank you," said Hannah and took it, feeling how ashamed the girl was.

"Thank you for doing your job," Lis added and winked at her before turning around.

As they went to the cashier, Hannah took her wallet out.

"No, no," Lisa pushed it back. "I'll pay."

"Why?" Hannah squinted her eyes from surprise.

"You gave me money remember?" Lisa said and pulled out the cash. "I owe you."

"Oh, come on, you can pay me back whenever."

"I want to do it now."

Lisa paid and gave the swimsuit to Hannah, clicking her tongue from excitement.

"Let's go!"

In half an hour, they stood in the changing room. The girls were chatting, dressed in all kinds of swimsuits: different colors, shapes, patterns. Hannah looked down at herself and then at others, feeling like a duckling between swans.

Everyone looks so good! she thought and peered at their shiny hair, smooth skin, and sparkling eyes.

"What are you waiting for?" Lisa's voice snapped her out of her train of thought. Hannah jerked as if newly awoken and looked at Lisa, wearing a red swimsuit and the shining material clasping around her body.

"You look so pretty!" Hannah exclaimed. Lis smiled and put her hair in a bun.

"Thanks," she said and pointed at the yellow bikini still lying next to Hannah. "I'll be waiting outside."

Hannah watched how every girl left the room, and after making sure she was alone, Hannah changed into the swimsuit. The size was a bit smaller, but it wasn't uncomfortable. Uncomfortable would be the eyes gawking at her when she'd appear.

After five minutes, when she stepped out, she distinguished some people stopping to talk and turning toward her to have a good look at Hannah. Feeling everyone's attention being drawn toward her, Hannah turned around, planning to go back but felt a grab of her arm.

"Where do you think you're going, beautiful?" Lisa cunningly whispered in her ear and pulled her closer.

Unable to resist her charm, Hannah followed her before she felt a kick from Lisa.

"What are you doing?" Hannah asked and laughed, seeing how she stood at the edge of the pool.

"Nothing," Lisa said and pushed her again.

"No!" Hannah laughed before Lisa pushed her more, and her feet slipped, but she wasn't going down alone. Hannah grabbed Lisa's arm tightly, so as she fell, she dragged Lisa too. Both of them splashed the water as they drowned and came back to the surface.

"You little devil!" Lisa laughed and splattered water on Hannah.

"You think I'd let you win?" Hannah replied and splashed the water back.

The girls giggled and played in the water; their voices echoed as they kept on, and Hannah had completely forgotten they weren't alone.

After two hours, Hannah and Lisa left the swimming pool with wet hair, the scent of chlorine, and drained energy. They came out in the hallway, still full of people - some coming from the gym, some leaving after training or swimming. Hannah felt how relaxed she was, how her muscles had softened, and her bones stopped aching. Everything about the day soothed her, both mentally and physically.

Suddenly, a familiar figure appeared in the crowd, and Hannah froze, seeing Chet stomping toward them, the sound of his shoes reverberating in the building. His creased brows and flushed cheeks exposed his frustration. Peeking at Lisa, Hannah noticed how her friend tensed up and prepared for the worst.

"What are you doing here?" Lisa asked as Chet rose in front of them with arms akimbo like a parent scolding a child.

"What am I doing here?" he yelled and snickered. "I've been calling you the whole day! Why didn't you answer me?"

"I was busy," Lisa replied. "And I don't have to let you know my every step anyway."

Chet fell quiet as a few of the people looked back at them. As Hannah's and his eyes met, she realized how much hate they were sated with.

"What's going on, Lisa?" he asked, now controlling the tone of his voice. "Are you pissed at me?"

"No," Lisa said and glanced at Hannah. "I just needed some time to think."

"Think about what?" Chet's frustration began coming back.

Lisa looked around and rolled her eyes. "Can't we talk about this later?"

"Later?" Chet exclaimed. "What are you doing now? Where are you going?"

This possessive side that Chet let slip out of his hard mask revealed his true self. Lisa's eyes enlarged, and she leaned back as if scared of the man standing before her.

"I'm going with Hannah," Lisa said and was about to turn toward her when Chet laughed out loud. He put his back and roared as if a wild creature crawled out of his stomach. Every voice halted, and people began staring curiously.

"Hannah?" he asked and looked at her with sarcasm. "This girl? This one, standing right beside you?" he questioned again, his voice heavy with irony.

"Yes, Hannah!" Lisa, horrified by the sudden shift of Chet's personality, exclaimed, glaring at him with widened eyes.

Hannah felt the familiar foreboding again while watching Chet standing before her, preparing to say something. His eyes kept sating with ridicule, and he continued sniggering as though not even noticing the people forming a circle around them.

"Look at her!" Chet finally let out a blasting voice that reached every corner, every ear. "Look at this ugly thing!" he continued and pointed at Hannah with both of his hands. "How can you even be her friend? She's the ugliest girl I've ever seen!"

Hannah felt anger building up inside her, but instead of giving in to the urge to punch Chet, she looked down. Shame and sadness changed her fury in a second, and all Hannah wanted was to hide away like a beetle under a rock. Tears escaped from her eyes, streaming down her face as Chet's words blared in her ears. She wanted to run away as fast as possible, but somehow she couldn't move her feet as if glued to the floor.

"Stop Chet!" Lisa yelled, but Chet ignored her.

"You're dumping me for her?!" he continued, laughing. "She's fat as a pig! She's so fucking ugly no man would want her. Aren't you embarrassed when you walk next to her?" he asked Lisa.

This was the last drop of Hannah's patience. Staring at her feet, she felt the eyes pinned on her, heard some chuckles and whispers. This was too much for Hannah even though she'd been living with humiliation. But now, as she stood next to Lisa and her boyfriend kept insulting her in front of everyone, Hannah felt how her soul died bit by bit inside her, how her heart shattered into pieces, and how her anxiety covered every other emotion. Her last traces of boldness vanished, and Hannah felt like a feeble animal. Cries of pain rushed to her mouth, and she pursed her lips to contain whaling.

Unable to bear more, Hannah worked her way through the crowd, running toward the entrance. Lisa's voice calling for her reached her, but Hannah didn't stop, feeling like she was running away from hell. But the situation was worse than hell - no physical torture could overweight the immense mental pain Hannah felt.

Running out in the streets, Hannah quickly passed by the people, trying to get home as soon as possible, wrap up in blankets and let the cries out. She felt like the world was crumbling down on her; the ground was cracking and dragging her into an abyss. The suffering was too much to handle as mental pain turned into physical pain, too: Hannah felt like her heart was being cut into pieces, and she felt every lance of the knife. She thought she could never come out of his dark hole of endless misery.

*

As the anger filled every vein in Lisa's body, she clenched her fists and gritted her teeth like a wolf preparing for a fight.

Only after Hannah left did Lisa realize that everyone had gathered around them, and some had even started recording videos. The humiliation Hannah had gone through was now in their phones, and Lisa could do nothing about it.

Her eyes skimmed over the people, finally freezing on Chet, who continued blabbering and laughing.

"Look how she ran away!" he roared. "Because she knows she's ugly."

"Shut up, Chet!" Lisa screamed, her fists tightening as her nails dug into her palms.

"Or what?" Chet shot back, gazing at her with sarcasm. "What are you going to do?"

From the corner of her eye, Lisa could still see people taking videos. Maybe she couldn't erase the old ones, but she could put a scene for a new video where Chet's embarrassment would overweight Hannah's. She had to do something to put her anger out, take revenge instead of her friend and make everyone shame Chet. He had already demeaned himself, but he needed to realize it too.

"What are you going to do, ha?" Chet continued, drawing closer to Lisa.

"This!" Lisa replied and shoved her fist into his nose.

The punch sent Chet reeling, and he fell on the ground, covering his nose with a hand. People gasped, their eyes jumping from Chet to Lisa and back.

Lisa waved his hand and massaged it, aching from the force she'd used. Chet, still sprawled on the floor, sat up, looking at Lisa with a horrified face. His eyes enlarged, doubled in size as if about to burst.

"What the hell," he mumbled and looked down on his palm, smudged with blood running from his nose, dribbling down his lips and white shirt.

"What? Are you surprise?" Lisa asked and spread her arms. "I saw the real you, and I thought you had to see real me too."

She licked her lips from satisfaction and walked up to him, standing and looking down on Chet as he lay on the floor.

"You are a piece of Chet," she snickered and threw the one last look of revulsion.

Lisa turned around, walking to one of the girls holding a phone. As she saw Lisa coming toward her, her smile vanished as if scared he'd get beaten up too. But Lisa pointed at her phone.

"You recorded this?" she said and looked at Chet, then back at the girl.

"Yes," the girl nodded with her hand trembling.

"Great!" Lisa exclaimed and smiled, turning back.

She stepped over Chet as if avoiding roadkill and walked to the entrance, feeling the eyes pinned on her back.

Lisa left the building with a proud smile. This smile would raise no doubt that she was delighted with her recent behavior and considered herself a winner, a girl who defended her friend in front of everyone and put true friendship before false love.

But as she left everyone behind and walked out in the streets, her smile vanished, and tears fell on her cheeks. Shaking her head, Lisa rubbed her face and hastened her steps. People kept staring at her, some even reaching out to ask if she was okay. Lisa avoided them and kept on walking wordlessly. She didn't know why she was crying. Maybe it was because of the humiliation Hannah had to go through that Lisa too felt as if she had been in her friend's shoes. Perhaps it was because her suspicions were true, and Chet wasn't the guy he pretended to be. Lisa confessed that she had some hope that Chet would turn out to be a kind person, and even though she didn't want to be with him, she hoped the time she'd spend with Chet she'd spend with a nice person.

How could I be so blind? Lisa asked herself, fighting the new tears.

Pursing her lips to contain whimper, Lisa crossed the street and ran into the building, then - up the stairs. She knew Hannah was in her room now, hiding in blankets and crying. This image squeezed Lisa's heart from pain, and she wiped her tears away, trying to stay strong for Hannah and herself too.

Lisa opened the door and stepped into the quiet apartment. As she closed it behind her back, she listened to the silence and distinguished stifled whimpers piercing it. Approaching Hannah's room, Lisa heard her voice and the sounds of cries became sharper. She knocked on it, and the cries halted.

"It's me," Lisa pleaded. "Can I come in?"

A long pause ensued before Hannah answered.

"Yeah, come in."

Walking inside, Lisa saw Hannah sitting on her bed, looking through the window. It seemed she had tried to clean her face from the ruined makeup, but black mascara was still smudged around her eyes. Her lips and cheeks had swelled from crying, and Lisa knew even though Hannah wasn't crying now, she was still holding in tears.

Gently sitting next to her, Lisa looked at Hannah and put her hand on hers.

"I'm sorry," Lisa let out, and Hannah shook her head.

"It's not your fault." Hannah's voice was husky, more gruff than usual.

"It is," Lisa said. "You told me you didn't like Chet, but I didn't believe that he was such a bad person. I didn't want to believe it."

Hannah licked her lips, still staring into the window. The fragments of blue sky peeked through the white clouds. The sun began setting; the night started replacing day.

"You know I punched Chet," said Lisa.

Surprised, Hannah looked at her with wide eyes.

"You did what?" she asked and chuckled. "while people recorded videos?"

"That's right," Lisa answered and shrugged. "I just couldn't leave without giving him what he deserved."

"You are crazy," Hannah said, and laughter burst out of her. "But he really deserved it."

"You should've seen his face," Lisa said and imitated Chet's shocked expression. "He couldn't believe his perfect girlfriend punched him. He was looking at me like I was a different person."

Hannah smiled sadly and glanced at the window again.

"You were a different person with him," she said. Lisa sensed that Hannah had wanted to say this for a long time, and she finally did.

"I know," Lisa sighed. "I was trying to be someone I am not."

They both fell quiet, listening to the sound of traffic and people coming from the streets. They sat silently, next to each other, holding hands.

*

Hannah felt emotions rushing into her, and tears began running down her face again, dribbling on her thighs. Lisa looked at her with a concerned face and gripped her hand tighter.

Hannah looked down, looking at their hands clenching each other as if they had no one else. And it was true. Hannah had no one but Lisa. She was her whole life, and without her, Hannah would stop existing.

She felt the emotions overswelling her, filling her body, trying to gush out from her pores. Hannah couldn't contain them anymore; it was out of her control. She'd been holding them inside for so many years, but her patience had reached its limit, and she felt like if she didn't let her feelings out, she would go crazy or die.

Licking her lips, Hannah wiped her tears and locked her eyes on Lisa, breathing heavily, preparing for a moment she'd been delaying for so long. It was now or never, she decided.

"What's wrong?" Lisa asked.

The words rushed to Hannah's mouth, and she opened it, letting them fly free for the first time.

"I'm in love with you," she said.

Waiting for Lisa's reaction, Hannah pursed her lips. She imagined Lisa shocked, surprised, or even disgusted. She imagined her jumping up and rushing off, leaving Hannah behind, or calmly rejecting her and saying there was nothing more than friendship between them. Hannah was ready for everything as she had already overstepped the most challenging obstacle and had confessed. Hannah wouldn't have to carry this weight anymore, and even if Lisa rejected her, she'd be better without keeping this secret that had been slowly eating her inside out.

But, to her surprise, Lisa smiled and softly put Hannah's hair behind her ear. Her warm palm brushed against her cheek, and Lisa's sweet smile grew, stars started twinkling in her eyes.

"I'm in love with you too," she let out.

As if unable to perceive her words, Hannah stared blankly at her. She thought she misheard it, or her mind was tricking her, making her hear what she'd yarned for.

"What?" Hannah finally asked, her face still loosened from surprise.

"I love you, Hannah," Lisa replied and leaned in, kissing her.

As Hannah felt Lisa's lips, she felt like she touched a soft feather. Lisa's plump, warm lips were put on hers, and Hannah couldn't help but kiss back.

"You believe now?" Lisa leaned back and smiled.

As if that kiss turned Hannah's brain on, the realization arrived, and she gasped, her face getting reddened and her eyes teary from happiness.

"Really?" she asked, her voice breaking.

"Yes, really," Lisa giggled and caressed her cheek. "But I thought," Hannah cleared her throat, even more, embarrassed at her clumsiness. "I thought you were straight."

"Turns out I'm not," Lisa winked. "You made me realize it."

Staring into her sparkling eyes, Hannah still couldn't believe that the girl she'd been in love with for so long was in love with her too. It seemed too perfect to be true.

"When did you realize it?" Hannah asked.

"A few weeks ago," Lisa responded and looked into space with reflective eyes. "I knew I didn't love Chet, but I also knew I loved someone else. It took me a while to realize it was you."

Now all the nervousness vanished from Hannah, and she

hugged Lisa, feeling their hearts beating in the same rhythm as if harmonizing.

How worthless all those self-doubts were, Hannah thought. She had spent so many years holding back from confessing and doubting Lisa's feelings.

Hannah leaned back, taking Lisa's face with her hands and gazing into her eyes for a while. As she did so, Lisa's features relaxed into delight, finally filling with desire. Her eyelids lowered, and her cheeks flushed, lips pouted forward unconsciously.

Hannah slowly kissed her. Now the kiss was passionate as both of them were aware of their feelings; both had accepted the reality, which was more beautiful than they had expected.

Her eyes closed; Hannah felt how Lisa opened her mouth, letting Hannah slip her tongue in. Lisa's hot tongue entangled with hers, and her lips got wet and swelled. Wrapping her arms around Lisa's waist, Hannah felt how her pulse raised from joy and love. Lisa, too wound her arms around Hannah's neck while they kissed slowly, letting themselves absorb every moment with each other.

The next day was sunnier than the previous one. Hannah and Lisa had just finished classes and headed toward a cafe to have some lunch. Holding her hand, Hannah felt how everything else became meaningless when she was Lisa. Filled with gratitude that she had her right by her side, Hannah clutched her hand and rested her head on Lisa's shoulder.

The heat reached its peak, and everyone tried to avoid the sun, searching for a cool place like homeless animals seeking shelter. The cafes were filled as people relaxed under air conditioners, sipping iced coffee. Even the birds had stopped flying, hiding from the sun under tree branches. The sweat crawling down people's necks would soon appear again after being wiped. Being in a busy city in July was too much torture, and everyone tried to deal with it in their own ways.

Hannah, too, felt her shirt soaking in sweat. Looking up at Lisa, she searched for a trace of wetness on her skin, but Lisa's face sparkled in clear white, without even a drop of sweat.

"How the hell aren't you hot?" Hannah gasped, making Lisa laugh.

"I am hot. I am very hot," Lisa winked with a cunning smile. "I just don't sweat."

"Are you an alien?" Hannah asked and glided her finger down Lisa's cheek. "You have a baby skin."

"I guess I am," Lisa replied and gave her a peck on the lips.

They walked into the cafe, giggling and chuckling. After buying two cups of coffee and pieces of chocolate cake, Hannah and Lisa sat at one of the tables. As Lisa took a bite, Hannah did the same, eating one after another. In a few minutes, when both of their plates were empty, Hannah realized that for the first time, she had eaten without taking people around her into consideration. She gazed at Lisa, sipping the coffee, and wondered how many powers Lisa had. Making Hannah forget her insecurities and enjoy the moment was one of them.

She really isn't an ordinary person; the thought crossed Hannah's mind. Maybe she isn't an alien, but she definitely is a superhero. My personal superhero.

"What are you smiling at?" Lisa's quirky voice revived her. She was looking at Hannah with pleasant embarrassment.

"You," Hannah responded honestly and put her hand on hers, resting on the table.

Giggling like a kid, Lisa caressed her cheek and hair, putting it behind Hannah's ear. Suddenly, from the corner of her eye, Hannah noticed a familiar presence, the one that brought no calm but anxiety. Turning her head, she saw Chet standing. It seemed he had just walked into the cafe and caught sight of Hannah and Lisa. His expression was heavy with disgust and loath.

Lisa stopped laughing and glared at him for a moment. Hannah thought that one of them would say something even though Chet didn't seem like he planned to apologize. Before Hannah could think more, Lisa grabbed her face and kissed her intensely as if they were alone. As they leaned back, Hannah saw how Chet chewed his lips from anger and turned around, dashing out of the cafe.

Entertained by Chet's reaction, Hannah and Lisa laughed, twinkling at each other. Holding her hand, Hannah realized that Lisa was hers, and she was Lisa's. Hannah had wasted so much time in doubts, but she knew she wouldn't waste even a minute more. They belonged to each other.

CHAPTER 5

The sky had grown light, and the silhouettes of high-rises shimmered in lilac under the orange-tinted clouds, floating above the city.

The streets were already busy, heavy with people of all kinds: students pattering with open books in their hands, sleeveless shirts revealing their arms, damp with sweat; Middle-aged people, dressed in suits and ties, rushing toward work, holding coffee cups and tablets; young mothers strolling with their babies dozing in their arms, soaking up the first sunlight.

Between all these people - everyone with their own worries and happiness, regrets and goals - walked Hannah and Lisa, no different from those around. But only one look at Hannah was enough to understand her thoughts: she thought no one in the whole world was as happy as her.

Hannah's eyes glimmered in bright as if the sun shone right through them, her smile spreading to its limit from delight, teeth shining under her lips and brows rising from overflowing joy. And all this was because of one thing - Lisa was her girlfriend.

Only the word girlfriend rose goosebumps on her arms. Lisa wasn't just a friend or best friend anymore. She had removed the label she'd been carrying for years and had stepped over the borders. Hannah still couldn't believe that the girl she'd been adoring, dreaming about, and calling a friend was now more than she'd ever been - they were dating, and it was enough for Hannah's happiness to reach its peak.

Holding Lisa's hand, Hannah looked at her, staring at her glowing skin and her hair swaying in the air.

She really is my girlfriend, Hannah thought. We really are

dating.

Hannah felt the urge to slap herself out of her daydreaming. But she wasn't dreaming - for the first time, her dreams had become a reality.

As they walked, Hannah thought that she and Lisa shone a light that separated them from the rest of the people, like some kind of holy figure. They were gleaming in yellow while others sunk in blackness. There was no one like them, as happy and in love as for them. That's what Hannah kept thinking, and her heart kept being filled with feelings that aimed to gush out of her. Even if someone jolted her, snickered, or threw a humiliating remark, Hannah wouldn't care. Now, all that mattered was her hand holding Lisa's and feeling her warmth.

"Hannah, stop that!" Lisa exclaimed and chuckled, shaking her head with her cheeks immediately flushing. They stopped, waiting for the streetlight to show green.

"Stop what?" Hannah asked, her eyes still glistening like stars reflecting on a lake surface.

"Staring at me with lovey-dovey expression," Lisa laughed, forgetting about the embarrassment and pinching Hannah's cheek.

"Ow, that hurt," revived by the pinch, Hannah pressed the reddened skin. "Okay, sorry."

Lisa smiled and looked ahead. Little devils began dancing in Hannah's head, which happened very rarely, but lately, as they had started dating, the devils began appearing more and more often.

"What is it? Do I make you uncomfortable?" she whispered in Lisa's ear with a sly tone of voice.

She noticed how hair rose to its end on Lisa's arms. She bit her lower lip, pink spreading on her cheeks again. Hannah chuckled as Lisa turned her head toward her and locked her eyes.

"Yes, you make me uncomfortable," she replied, her voice not less cunning than Hannah's. "But in a good way."

Lisa leaned in, her lips slowly drawing toward Hannah's, finally gently touching them and then moving up and down. Hannah's head followed the motion, going back and forth. With her eyes closed, Hannah fully immersed into the kiss as if there was no one around. A wall rose between them and the rest of the world. Lisa and Hannah had their own world where they found complete serenity and love.

Surrounded by people waiting to cross the street, Hannah and Lisa kept kissing. A few heads turned toward them, a few offended eyes of old ladies or curious gaze of children. But Hannah didn't care. Not anymore since they'd been dating for about a month now. At first, when Lisa had tried to kiss her in public, Hannah had panicked and rejected her. But after a few times of Lisa taking her face and kissing her anyway, saying how everyone who felt uncomfortable could go to hell, Hannah had begun fighting her insecurity too. And finally, she got used to it. So much so that now she initiated kissing Lisa in streets, cafes, or college.

The streetlights lit up in green, and Hannah and Lisa snapped out of their passion, crossing the street, still holding each other's hands. It seemed like they never let go as if trying to make up for all those years they'd wasted.

Soon, they reached a small cafe under the shadow of broad pine trees. They took seats outside, ordering iced coffee and ice cream. The sunlight reached through the green leaves, scattering into thin golden strings, twinkling on Lisa's face.

"Do you know what's that called?" Hannah asked as Lisa giggled at the sunlight dancing on her forehead. "Komorebi. In Japanese."

"What?" Lisa asked with a smile.

"The sunlight reaching through trees," Hannah put her hand under the light lining the table surface, then glanced up at Lisa. "It's beautiful as you."

A smile of amazement formed across Lisa's face. She glided her fingertips down Hannah's arm.

The waitress brought coffee and ice cream in glasses. Lisa poured a bit of coffee onto the ice cream and took a scoop.

"You're so weird," Hannah laughed.

"Look who's talking," Lisa raised her brows and offered a

spoon full of her coffee-mixed ice cream. "Taste it."

Opening her mouth, Hannah let Lisa put the spoon inside, and she swallowed the cream, licking her lips.

"Good, right?" Lisa smiled with a winner's face.

"Yeah," Hannah nodded, chuckling at Lisa's childish sense of competition.

"It's good we took summer classes," Lisa said as both of them had finished eating, the plates completely clean. "We'll have extra credits."

"Yeah, and we can go to a beach in August or September," Hannah nodded. "Nowhere's boring with you anyway."

Hannah put her hand on the table, and Lisa grabbed it immediately, like a kid tugging onto the edge of her mother's skirt. Hannah beamed at her.

"I still can't believe we are dating," she confessed and laughed at how unreal her words sounded.

"Believe it," Lisa squeezed her hand, her eyes soothing as though honey was pouring out of them. "This is our life."

Hannah nodded, letting happiness take over her. It was time to stop overthinking, doubting, and fearing the future. It was time to start enjoying the moment and let herself love and be loved. A smile rose to her lips. Hannah realized she had just started truly living.

Hannah and Lisa spent the whole day outside, strolling or sitting in the park, kissing and talking. That was another thing Hannah loved about Lisa: with her, she could talk about everything that came to her mind, no matter how embarrassing, shameful or meaningless it was. Lisa never judged; on the contrary, she always tried to understand Hannah. At the end of the conversation, Hannah was often surprised at how much she and Lisa had in common.

The day had reached its end, and Hannah and Lisa headed for home, walking down the street, holding hands. The streetlights shimmered on the dark streets, lined up like artificial stars. People had scattered, everyone toward their homes, exhausted from the long day, ready to curl up on beds and sink into slumber. The calm night sky looked like a mourning dress of a beautiful woman. The trees gently rocked back and forth as the zephyr blew through them.

Holding Lisa's hand, Hannah looked up at the sky, noticing a few stars illuminating in faded silver.

"Look, it's so pretty," she said, and Lisa's eyes followed the direction.

"It really is," she murmured, gazing at the little dots on the sky as white paint dribbled on black canvas. "We rarely see the stars."

"Today's a special night," Hannah said and looked at her. Lisa's and her eyes met, and they gently kissed. Every night was special when they were together.

But the time had passed 12, and they had to go to bed to wake up for morning classes. As Lisa opened the apartment door, they walked into the darkened room, and Lisa closed the door behind. Hannah stopped, waiting for Lisa to make a move, thinking maybe it was the right time, that maybe they could overstep their limits and finally do more than kissing. But Lisa looked down and walked up to her room.

"Good night, Hannah," she whispered, her face drowning into the gloom. She had rested her right hand on the open door as if contemplating going inside.

Hannah stood in the doorway of her room, she too, leaning on the wall. Lisa's eyes lingered on her for a moment, and Hannah read the apology in them. Lisa was ashamed of being unable to take the step.

"Don't worry," Hannah said with a soothing tone. "The time will come."

Lisa smiled and nodded before going into her room. Hannah did the same, rolling on the empty bed and closing the coverlet above her head.

It had been a month, but they had decided to take it slow. There was no need to hurry and move on as other couples did. Hannah kept saying that too, but she felt like the time had stretched too long, and the wait became a bit unbearable. She wanted Lisa, and she knew Lisa wanted her too. But there was a boundary between them that kept them from getting closer to each other: that might have been inexperience in having relationships - both romantical and sexual. None of them, not Lisa or Hannah, had ever had serious relationships, only glimpses of them that had last a few days or weeks. They had never seemed to find the person who would stick longer. And now that they had finally found one, surprisingly the person who'd been by their side all those years, they didn't know what to do. Hannah wasn't less confused than Lisa, and she confessed - she was scared too. But one thing that intensified Lisa's hesitation was that she had never been interested in a girl. This was very new to her.

Exhausted from the train of thought, Hannah turned to her side, facing the window and staring out of it. The stars like little crystals glistened in the sky, and she questioned if Lisa watched them too. Spreading her hands on the bed, Hannah wondered for how long would she have to sleep in an empty bed.

*

The ticking of her watch became more and more fierce as the teacher kept reading from the book and walking up and down the aisles of desks. The heat had piled up in the room, heaving down the students, making it hard to breeze. The open windows didn't help as they let the heat come in from outside. Wondering why didn't they turn the AC on, Hannah looked at the wall, finding out that they had no AC at all. Sighing, she looked down at her watch. Only one minute was left for the class to end, but the minute felt like an hour. Hannah pinned her eyes on the hand on the watch, feeling like its movements slowed down every second, and instead of nearing 12, it distanced from it further.

Finally, the teacher stopped talking, and before she could say goodbye, the students jumped up, ramming into the door, leaving one by one. Hannah, too, rushed out and then down the hall, seeing Lisa waiting for her and scrolling through her phone.

She smiled at Hannah and turned the phone off.

"You were waiting for me?" Hannah asked and squeezed the books into her bag.

"Yeah, of course. You aren't the only one waiting," Lisa replied, winking at her.

They came out of the building, and as Lisa spread her hand to hold Hannah's, she instinctively put it back. Peering around her, Hannah got scared the students would start picking on them, calling names as they'd see them holding hands.

"Their studies opinions don't matter," said Lisa, seemingly reading Hannah's mind. "We are in love, and we hold hands. What's so unusual about it?"

Hannah inhaled, trying to force the doubts to the back of her head, and took Lisa's hand. As she did so, she felt home; she felt secure as if not even the strongest forth could harm her, as though she would leave any fight without a scratch.

"What should we do today?" Lisa asked as they began strolling down the path toward the gates.

"Let's stay inside and turn on the AC," said Hannah. "Maybe watch a movie or something."

"Sounds good," Lisa smiled at her.

Hannah didn't realize how they walked through the open gates as she was sinking into Lisa's deep eyes. Only after they reached home did she snap out of it and perceived that they had crossed the entire college yard and no one had said a word.

Hannah tapped the pencil on the book, her eyes quickly skimming the pages from edge to edge. She yawned and looked up, seeing Lisa napping next to her, her head flopped on the open book. Hannah chuckled, watching how Lisa slept soundly, hands under her cheeks, like a little kid listening to a lullaby.

Hannah caressed her cheek, noticing how Lisa scrunched up her nose, then slowly opened her eyes.

"Oh, sorry, I woke you up," Hannah apologized and was about to put her hand back when Lisa caught it and put it back on her hair. Smiling, Hannah continued caressing Lisa's head.

"Ah, it feels so good," Lisa let out a moaning sound. As she realized it, she pursed her lips and gawked at Hannah with an embarrassed expression.

A bit startled, Hannah stopped her movements; she, too, realized how erotic Lisa's voice had sounded.

Suddenly, she caught a glimpse of the laptop lying behind Lisa, and an idea formed in her mind. She glanced at Lisa and then back at the computer.

"What is it?" sensing Hannah deep into her thoughts, Lisa asked and sat up.

Licking her lips, Hannah hesitated, saying her thoughts aloud, as if verbalizing them would make them come true.

"I thought we could watch something," she began with a playful tone but then got serious, afraid Lisa wouldn't have the same reaction.

"What?" Lisa asked, still confused.

"Porn," Hannah replied.

Within a second, redness emerged on Lisa's face, and she looked back at the laptop.

"Are you sure?" she asked. "Won't it be awkward?"

"Maybe," Hannah shrugged. "But perhaps it will help us, you know..." she cleared her throat. "Take that step we've been trying to take."

Lisa fell into thoughts for a few seconds, searching Hannah's face.

"Okay," she agreed and, to Hannah's surprise, jumped up, grabbing the laptop.

They went into Lisa's room and sat on the bed, a bit awkwardly - straightened backs and hands neatly placed in laps as if waiting for a class to start.

"Do you know a site?" Lisa asked.

"Yeah, I do," Hannah said and scoffed. "You don't?"

Lisa tutted and jolted her before Hannah logged in to a site, searching for Lesbian sex. She was used to watching them, but it was new to Lisa, and it showed on her face: her eyes widened, and she swallowed, at first avoiding looking at the screen but then peeping at it, curiosity getting best of her.

The video started, and Hannah leaned back, her arm touching Lisa's. In the video, the girls began kissing, slowly but passionately. Then one of them pushed the other down and began kissing down her back, licking and biting from time to time.

"Wow, you know the best porn out there, don't you?" Lisa mentioned, partly trying to break the silence.

Hannah chuckled and continued watching the video that became more and more erotic every second. Soon the girls' moans filled the room as one of them slipped fingers inside the other.

Hannah felt how her breath shortened, and her underwear became wet. Peering toward Lisa, she noticed how her expression had changed. Now Lisa wasn't ashamed but aroused, biting her lips and swallowing, breathing sharply.

Hannah felt the wetness growing between her legs, and she couldn't contain the heaving anymore. Suddenly, she felt Lisa's hand crawling up her waist, and as she turned her head toward Lisa, she saw her eyes sinking into lust. She was hungry for Hannah. They both opened their mouths, and Lisa pushed the laptop away. Hannah rolled above Lisa, running her fingers through her hair, sliding her tongue inside her mouth. Lisa let out quiet moans, and as she leaned back, the saliva stretched into a thread between their lips.

Looking down on Lisa, Hannah felt the desire pushing her from inside like a living creature. Lisa's pink face screamed with ardor, and she put her head up, asking for more.

Hannah slowly stripped Lisa of her clothes, and Lisa did the same, her hot fingertips gliding on Hannah's skin, making electricity ran down her body. Finally, both of them were naked, and for the first time, Hannah had forgotten all about her weight. Lisa wound her arms around her, licking her neck and then gliding her tongue down, finally sucking on Hannah's nipple while rubbing the other. Hannah let groans of pleasure leave her mouth, feeling Lisa's soft lips around her nipples. Hannah slid her hand down Lisa's stomach, moving on the smooth skin and reaching her crotch. As Hannah's fingers slithered her clitoris, Lisa breathed in, holding it for a few seconds. As she let the air out, she moaned, and Hannah worked her fingers inside her, feeling how soaked Lisa was.

"Open your legs," said Hannah, surprised by her own voice as if listening to a stranger. Her voice had never sounded so heavy with fervor.

Lisa obeyed, and Hannah sat on top of her, their clitoris touching each other. As Lisa moaned, Hannah sucked her lips, her voice halting into the kiss. Then she pushed Lisa's right leg up, placing it on her shoulder while she kept riding, moving her hips back and forth. Feeling her blood boiling, Hannah let her body follow the impulses, and she heard the bed hitting the wall, making a loud sound. Lisa grabbed her hands while both screamed from pleasure. Hannah and Lisa continued sinking into a fire of lust deeper and deeper with their fingers entangled, finally reaching the orgasm together.

Lisa's body trembled, and she gasped as Hannah froze for a second, immersing herself in the intense pleasure. Exhaling, she flopped over, falling on the bed next to Lisa. Still breathing heavily as if she'd been running for hours, Lisa looked at Hannah with a broad smile.

"Damn, that was good," she said with a tired voice. "No. It was great. Perfect"

Hannah smiled and turned on her side. Lisa did the same, so they looked straight into each other's eyes.

"You really liked it?" Hannah asked.

"Are you kidding?" Lisa laughed. "This was the best sex I've ever had."

Pleased with the answer, Hannah kissed her and wiped the sweat crawling down Lisa's forehead.

"Everything was perfect," Lisa murmured and pushed the coverlet above their damp, tired, relaxed bodies. Then she furled in an embryo pose and put her head on Hannah's chest.

"I love you," she whispered, her voice revealing she was already half asleep.

"I love you too," Hannah replied and put her arms over her.

The quiet humming of the AC sounded like an abstract melody, flowing into Hannah's ears. The cool air glided on her skin and made Lisa's curls, spread on the bed, flutter. The night slowly settled into the city and brought quiet, replacing the heat and noise of the day.

A smile slowly danced on Hannah's lips as she let her heavy eyelids close, listening to Lisa sleeping. A thought arrived that those years spent with unrequited love, all those difficulties, and all those heartbreaks or jealousy she had to experience worth it, for only to sleep with Lisa in her arms.

It was all worth it; the thought flashed in her mind before Hannah finally gave in slumber.

The sunlight crept inside and glistened on the walls. Rolling over in bed, Hannah swished her hand over on the pillow, unconsciously searching for Lisa's body but ran into emptiness. Peeling her eyelids from one another, Hannah saw a bundled-up blanket and the hollow in the pillow created by Lisa's head. It seemed she had just got up. Hannah looked around, but she was alone in the room.

Looking down on herself and noticing her naked body wrapped in the coverlet, Hannah recalled the previous night. As the memories came flooding back, Hannah giggled and shook her head, still seeing Lisa's fervid face and hearing the sound of her heaving.

Hannah flopped back on the bed, realizing she was in Lisa's bedroom, and it made her happiness grow and overflow.

I'm sleeping in her bed, she thought. *Totally naked.*

Giggling again, Hannah sprawled and sniffled the blankets. Everything reeked of Lisa and her sweet odor.

Suddenly she felt a premonition. Scared that Lisa regretted the previous night, Hannah set up, thinking that would be the reason she had left the bed so early in the morning. Hannah jumped up, throwing on an oversized shirt and running out.

"Lisa did you-" she began but froze to the spot.

Lisa stood with her back to Hannah, talking to a woman. As the woman saw Hannah, she leaned to her right to take a good look at the girl.

"Oh, hi Hannah," she said with a shrill voice. "How are you?"

"Hello, Ms. Hobbs," Hannah stumbled over her words. Lisa's mother stood right in front of her, and she didn't know what to do.

Lisa looked back with vexed expression as if apologizing to Hannah for something she had no control over.

"I was just talking to Lisa about how I caught the last train and came here," said her mother, took off her red silk gloves and neatly placed them on the table.

"Why didn't you call me, Samantha?" Lisa asked and sighed, falling onto the couch and crossing her legs. She looked up at Hannah and then looked forward, everywhere but at her mother as if trying to avoid her face.

Hannah still stood in the doorway with only the long shirt on, feeling embarrassed about her completely naked body, the shirt covered.

"Why? Aren't you happy I visited you?" said Samantha and looked around in the room with a scowl on her face.

"I just preferred we were prepared."

"So, you could tidy this place up a bit?" Samantha let out and put her hair up in a bun. "It's a total mess."

There were no dirty plates piled up in the sink or empty packages of snacks scattered around, but Samantha still stared with a disgusted look.

Hannah sneaked into her room and quickly put on the clothes. When she went back into the living room, Samantha had already put on a water boiler and cut up an apple.

Hannah sat beside Lisa and heard her muffled growls that Lisa tried to trap inside her throat. Putting her hand on Lisa's, Hannah looked at her with sympathetic eyes, but she put her hand back the moment Samantha turned around.

Looking at the woman elegantly eat the tiny pieces of an apple, Hannah realized that she never changed. Samantha looked and acted the same way she did twenty years ago. Something in her was vampiric, almost robotic as her skin never wrinkled, her hair never went grey, or her body never lost those firm muscles.

Hannah observed Samantha's white face and full lips colored with rich red, long blonde hair joined in a bun, light pink shirt, and classical trousers emphasizing her flattering figure. Lisa looked like her in appearance, but their personalities had nothing in common. While Lisa was a free soul, Samantha lived within the borders of rules she had created for herself.

Samantha and Lisa's father divorced when Lisa was only 3, and since then, Hannah had never seen Samantha with a man as if she had given up on love, romance and sex. Samantha had always been saying she would always be a single mother and dedicate her life to her only child, but it never seemed that way. Lisa spent days outside while Samantha went to salons and shops. She dedicated her life not to Lisa but to her beauty as the thought of losing it scared her to death. And she preserved it quite well, not letting her skin wrinkle by ignoring all her problems.

Lisa never liked her mother and often said she wished she lived with Hannah and her loving family. Avoiding seeing her mother was a way for her to hate her less. If she didn't see her, she didn't have to deal with her. That's why Lisa got so annoyed when Samantha arrived unannounced, pretending to be a caring mother - something she had never been.

"What are your plans for today?" Samantha asked and poured coffee for herself.

"I don't know," Lisa didn't try to hide the ire in her voice. "We have classes and then gotta do homework."

"Let's go to a restaurant tonight, three of us," Samantha suggested with her jovial, high-pitched voice. "We will have a great dinner and drink a little, listen to live music. What do you think?"

Lisa glanced at Hannah with squinted eyes, begging for help, but there was no way out of the situation.

"I'll take the silence as a yes," Samantha exclaimed and grabbed her purple suitcase, too big for a one-day trip.

"It's the white door," said Lisa, pointing at it.

Samantha nodded and stepped inside when she suddenly froze and turned on her heels.

"Didn't Hannah came out of here today?" she asked, her eyes jumping from Lisa to Hannah and back.

They glanced at each other, and Hannah got confused, her thoughts entangling.

"We were watching a movie last night and fell asleep," Lisa quickly said.

Hannah peeped toward her, surprised at how innocent and genuine her words sounded. When it came to necessity, Lisa could lie quite easily.

Samantha nodded and went into the room, closing the door. They heard the sound of her suitcase unzipping.

Lisa stood up, rubbing her face with her palms and pacing up and down.

"Ugh, this is the last thing I needed right now," she let out.

Hannah stood up, trying to touch her shoulders, but Lisa didn't stop, still walking in circles.

"She'll leave tonight; it's not that big of a deal," said Hannah.

Lisa stopped, drooping her shoulders in a hunch.

"You know how she is," she said with an exhausted voice. "She'll soon begin judging me and my life. She'll make me snap."

"Don't listen to her," Hannah held her hands and leaned in. They put foreheads against each other and looked into the eyes. "We'll get through it together."

Lisa pouted her lips, and Hannah couldn't help but kiss, sinking into them like in a pillow of feathers. Suddenly, the doorknob rustled, and they jumped from each other as if turning into grasshoppers.

"Your room is a mess," said Samantha as she walked out, now wearing a light green dress with dangling golden earrings.

Hannah felt how Lisa tensed up. She rushed into her room, passing by and jolting Samantha with her shoulder.

"I gotta get ready," Lisa mumbled, slamming the door.

Samantha tutted and looked back at Hannah, who shrugged awkwardly and walked toward her room. Suddenly she felt pity toward Samantha. Maybe she was trying to give her daughter the attention she had never given her; perhaps she was trying to become a good mother. It was late but, as it's said - better late than never.

"She's just tired," said Hannah before going into her room, coming up with an excuse for Lisa's behavior.

Samantha smiled weakly at her and slightly nodded. Both of them knew Hannah was saying a white lie.

"Thanks, Hannah," she muttered. "Thanks for saying what I want to hear."

She stood with a thin smile for a moment before walking into the kitchen. In a second, Hannah heard the low sound of Samantha humming the song she always sang quietly when she was irritated - "Can't Smile Without You" by Barry Manilow. Realizing it wouldn't be an easy day, Hannah let out a sigh and went into her room.

*

Something kept nibbling on Lisa's heart, like hungry worms gnawing on fallen leaves. Inhaling, she clutched her chest, rubbing her palm as if trying to numb the pain. Even the glimpse of thought about her mother pierced her mind like a sharp blade thrusting her head. She needed to come up with an excuse to avoid going to the restaurant. She couldn't sit there in a fancy dress, eating overprices food, looking at her dolled-up mother. She just couldn't.

Her eyes sneaking toward the window while the teacher's voice became distant; Lisa licked her lips, feeling the tears welling up. How could she say she didn't love her mother when she did. But even loving her felt like a crime when Samantha didn't care about Lisa at all.

She doesn't deserve my love. Lisa mused.

Samantha was everything but her mother. Lisa could call her a relative, a stranger, a woman with obsessions, a person she knew the best, a lady who abandoned her as a child without actually leaving her, but - never a mother.

Lisa tried to remember the last time she had called Samantha mom. She couldn't. Her lower lip started trembling, and she pursed them. She had always dreamed of a caring, loving, supportive mother who'd make her breakfast, kiss her cheek before leaving for work, and brush her hair in the mornings. Lisa had never experienced any of them. That's why she always wished she were Hannah's mother's daughter. Lisas's whole childhood was waiting for her mother in front of the TV while Samantha spent days away, leaving her kid all alone. That's what Samantha reminded Lisa of - utter loneliness, the sound of cartoons lancing silence, and the night breeze filling an empty room.

"Are you okay?" Hannah's voice threw her back to the present. As if drowning in a pool of her past, Lisa gasped, the air rushing in her lungs. Looking at Hannah, she felt serenity washing over her. She was right here, right now, with Hannah by her side. She would be okay.

"Yeah," Lisa nodded and smiled, noticing how students had started getting up to leave the classroom.

"Is the class over?" Lisa asked, grabbing her bag.

"Yeah," Hannah replied, searching her face. "Are you really okay?"

"Yeah, don't worry," Lisa smiled at her, realizing that the teacher's every word had slipped through her mind while she kept thinking about Samantha.

They went outside, Hannah holding Lisa's hand and rubbing her palm with her thumb.

"Are you nervous about tonight?" she asked slowly, carefully choosing her words. "About the dinner."

Lisa sighed, letting out the air piling up inside her and making it hard to swallow.

"I have a bad feeling about it," she confessed. "I don't want to go."

Hannah caressed her palm again, and even this subtle movement made Lisa feel a little bit less anxious. She wondered if Hannah had some kind of magical electricity in her hands or was this just the effect of immense love filling both of them.

"Maybe if we say we have a lot of homework, she'll leave us alone," Lisa suggested, the uneasiness coming back as soon as her thoughts went back to Samantha.

"But she hasn't seen you since we got in college," Hannah's voice sounded tender but eager, trying to convenience Lisa. "I feel like she's really trying this time."

"You think?" Lisa scrunched her brows, gazing at Hannah. For a moment, she thought she should've considered her words. Hannah was the smartest and most sensible person she knew.

Hannah nodded. "Give her a chance."

"How many times?" Lisa asked, shaking her head in dismay but looked over at Hannah again, whose eyes were pinned on her. Maybe Hannah was telling the truth or just trying to bring peace as she always did. Either way, Lisa felt like she should've agreed. "Okay, let's go."

Hannah smiled, leaning toward Lisa, brushing against her arm like a cat sweeping against warm ground under the morning light. The warmth of her body spread on Lisa's, and she put her hand around Hannah's waist, letting her exhausted body rely on her. As they walked, Lisa felt like Hannah shared her weight, so heavy and so hard to carry by shoulders. But right beside Hannah, Lisa felt the weight lightening. She knew Hannah would always share Lisa's share of worries, whole life.

The sound of glasses and forks clinking rang in Lisa's ears as she sat at the round table, tugging on the edge of the white table-cloth. The smell of the food made the sickening feeling rise in her; the chatter of people and the wine sparkling in the round glasses perfectly matched the atmosphere of an expensive restaurant.

Samantha lightly moved the knife across the stake as the blood trickled from it, spreading on the plate. The feeling turned into an unbearable urge to vomit, and Lisa gulped the water, taking her eyes off of the stake. She felt Hana's hand snaking on hers and squeezing it under the table.

"Isn't this place amazing?" Samantha asked, chewing the meat as her eyes skimmed the place. She had changed her outfit again, wearing a long blue dress dotted with white flowers with long silver earrings and curled hair.

Lisa didn't answer, sipping the water again.

"Yes, it's nice," Hannah replied instead of her.

Samantha swallowed, looking down with a disgruntled look.

"Thanks for answering, Hannah," she said. "My daughter seems to have forgotten how to talk."

Blood started boiling inside her as Lisa gritted her teeth, about to burst into yells. But suddenly, a waiter appeared out of the thin ear with a bottle of wine in his hand.

"Would you like more?" he asked politely. Tension piled up above their heads.

"Yes, please," Samantha smiled and raised her empty glass. The waiter filled it up and slowly vanished like smoke.

Samantha sipped the wine, her eyebrows rising, her face reddening from the alcohol in her body.

"Maybe you've had enough," Lisa said through her gritted teeth.

"And maybe you've been mean enough," Samantha shot back.

Lisa inhaled, locking her eyes on her mother. The person looking back at her seemed completely strange, unfamiliar, unknown. Lisa didn't know who she was gazing at. She realized she couldn't do this anymore.

"I've gotta go," she said and put down the napkin spread on her lap. "I've got an early practice tomorrow."

"You still play that?" Samantha clicked her tongue, her knife slicing the meat. "Won't you better study instead of playing those childish games?"

Lisa felt her anger rushing up to her head as if trying to burst it open. She bumped on the table and growled at Samantha like a wolf prepared for a fight.

"You don't get to talk to me like that," she almost whispered, her lips quivering.

"Why? I'm just saying that you are wasting your time,"

Samantha continued, ignoring the fury twisting Lisa's face. "You won't ever have a career out of playing sports. It's time you forget those dreams of yours and start thinking realistically."

Lisa felt her insides turning upside down, tears welling up in her eyes. She was about to jump up and break into screams when suddenly Hannah's voice stopped her.

"You don't know your daughter, Ms. Hobbs," she said with a loud, steady voice, clear as a bell ringing. She gazed at Samantha, who stared back, surprised. "Do you know she's a top basketball player at college? Do you know that she's already had offers from one of the most successful teams in the country? Do you know that the whole college is her fan?"

Samantha's eyes narrowed, and shame ran across her face. She slightly shook her head.

"Lisa is the most brilliant person I know," Hannah continued and squeezed her hand. "And if you can't see it, you don't deserve a second of her attention."

Tears rolled down Lisa's face as Hannah looked at her with a smile. She had never felt so protected; no one had stood up for her like this. Now, as she listened to Hannah, Lisa knew she would always be safe by Hannah's side.

She wiped off the tear, a smile splitting her lips.

"And we are dating!" Lisa exclaimed and kissed Hannah, ignoring Samantha's eyes widening.

Both of them stood up, looking at Samantha with the winners' faces.

"And today morning Hannah came out of my room because we had sex last night!" Lisa added, noticing few heads turning their way. Redness flashed on Samantha's face, and she swallowed from embarrassment, still gawking at Lisa and Hannah.

"Let's go," Lisa turned to her girlfriend, putting her arm over Hannah's shoulder. "She can eat alone. She doesn't need me. She never did."

They turned around, leaving Samantha and the scent of wine and food behind, stepping out into the fresh air. Lisa breathed it in, feeling the shackles slipping from her hands.

As they stepped into the apartment, Lisa twirled like an animal newly escaped from a cage. She felt free, free of her mother and her rules.

"Thank you so much!" she let out and ran up to Hannah, who giggled.

"I said what I was thinking," she shrugged.

"That's why I love you so much!" Lisa hugged her, sniffling Hannah's neck and the subtle scent of lavender. "You are always so honest without even realizing how much effect you have."

They stood in the empty room, hugging each other. Lisa felt Hannah's heartbeat getting faster.

"I'm sorry," Hannah mumbled.

"For what?" Lisa chuckled, looking at Hannah's face. She looked down, regret forming in her black eyes.

"I shouldn't have made you go to the dinner."

"Oh, come on," Lisa caressed her cheek, and Hannah closed her eyes as if feeling the warmth of her palm. "You didn't know."

"I really thought she tried to change," Hannah muttered.

Lisa sighed. "She never does, and I'm used to it."

Then she leaned in, kissing Hannah. At first, the kiss was soft, gentle, as if Lisa showed her gratitude through it. But in a second, as though flames appeared around them, Lisa felt her body burning from desire, and as she opened her eyes, she saw Hannah's face - red and eager to have Lisa all to herself.

They wound arms around each other, bodies entangling as if melting into each other. Lisa slid her hand under Hannah's pants, soon listening to the soft moans fondling her ears. Hannah's hands crawled under Lisa's shirt, cupping her breasts and massaging the nipples. The nerves gathered up in the two spots began tensing and trembling while Hannah kept rubbing Lisa's nipples and gasping as Lisa continued moving her hand up and down in her pants.

Lisa stepped forward and pushed Hannah into her room, both of them flopping on her black sheets. As Lisa realized they were in Hannah's room where everything reeked of her, Lisa's enthusiasm grew stronger. She grabbed Hannah's shirt, almost ripping it off of her, then removing her bra, exposing Hannah's heavy breasts. Lisa felt the wetness spreading inside her, and she kissed Lisa while pressing her crotch on Hannah's and moving up and down, sliding fingers inside her. Unable to contain the moans, she let them out, noticing Hannah's eyes had closed from the ecstasy.

"Look at me," Lisa said and touched her chin. "I want to see your eyes when you come."

Opening them, Hannah swallowed before her mouth took an o shape. Lisa's features trembled from pleasure, and they gazed at each other as the orgasm took over them.

Panting, Lisa sprawled on top of Hannah, resting her head on her chest that still kept rapidly moving.

"Ah, that was hot," Hannah let out with a chuckle.

"It was," Lisa agreed, then put her head up. Sweat beads had formed on Hannah's forehead. "Wanna try sex toys next time?"

"Oh, you already want to experiment?" Hannah giggled, gliding her hand down Lisa's hair.

"Why not?" Lisa smiled. "It'll be fun."

"Okay," Hannah laughed and dropped her head on the pillow.

Lisa exhaled, smile still curving her lips. Samantha had completely left her mind, now sinking in peace and quiet. Feeling Hannah's skin against hers, her hand gently moving along her spine, and the scent of her sweat, Lisa closed her eyes. She didn't need anyone if she had Hannah.

CHAPTER 6

The sun blazed down on the spectators gathered around the basketball court as they kept cheering for the upcoming game. The floor shone in red and brown as the white nets of the baskets swayed in the zephyr. The sound of people became louder as they couldn't contain the impatience anymore. The crumbs of popcorn and hotdogs scattered between the chairs, soda spilling everywhere. Onlookers had taken their seats, the tension and excitement piling up around the court as it stayed empty. No one could wait till the players would stomp on it, leaving the traces of their sneakers on the clean court.

Hannah sat in the first row on a chair that Lisa had gotten for her. It was one of the most important games, and Hannah, of course, couldn't miss it. Even though she had no doubt Lisa's team would win, she still had noticed her girlfriend's nervousness in the morning. Lisa was never anxious before a game, but she had never wanted to win so much. The victory would mean a lot to her team and the college.

Hannah's eyes gleamed as she skimmed the surroundings. Not only the students had gathered, but also their friends. Hannah couldn't recognize half of them. Their eyes sparkling with excitement revealed their thoughts - they didn't even consider losing. It was a fight between two colleges, and Lisa's team had to win the war - there was no alternative.

Suddenly the screams got louder, and people jumped on their feet, clapping and welcoming the players with cheerful sounds. They ran on the court, waving at the fans. Lastly, Lisa appeared, and the ovation exceeded the limits. Hannah felt like her ears would burst, but she was nothing but happy that so many people loved Lisa. They had no other choice - everyone fell in love with her the moment they met her.

Hannah kept on clapping as Lisa looked toward her. Through her wide smile, Hannah could discern signs of worry.

"You can do it, Lisa," Hannah mumbled. "You will win."

As if able to hear her whispers, Lisa's smile grew, and she waved at her before standing with her team. The red uniform adorned her body, her golden curls - braided behind her head. The delicate glow of her skin made her look like a nymph sliding from underwater.

As the green team arrived, the game began. The people kept cheering and gasping, booing when the green team gained a score but never let the red team feel their disappointment. Gazing at Lisa, Hannah saw how she became more and more nervous, her features quivering as the opponents got close to their basket. Hannah kept clapping and trying to let her know she was there for her no matter what, but Lisa was completely immersed in a game - now only she and the ball existed.

In two hours, the game approached the end. Both the spectators and the players were soaked in sweat. Everyone fidgeted on their feet, chewing on their fingertips from nervousness as Lisa stood with the ball in her hand, a few feet from the basket. Only one point was crucial - Lisa would throw the ball in the basket, and her team would win; she'd miss, and they would lose.

The tension growing roots inside everyone made the people fall quiet. Hannah could hear their heartbeats as their eyes were pinned on Lisa. The silence felt like a heavy cloud shrouding the court.

She peered toward her, noticing the pressure tightening around Lisa. Her body tensed, and her jaws clenched. She knew the victory depended on her, and the last thing Lisa wanted was to disappoint herself and her fans.

Hannah watched how a strange force rose in Lisa as if another creature woke up in her. Her body loosened like a feather in the wind. Her features stopped shaking, and her eyelids lowered. Composure washed over her, and in a second, she threw the ball.

As soon as the ball left Lisa's fingers, the spectators glanced at the basket. It felt like the ball flew in the air forever, but when it finally reached the destination, people realized every sweat and tear was worth it - the ball slid in the basket, gliding through the nest like a fish even without shaking it.

Everyone yelled from relief, and their palms began reddening as their clapped with all their energy. Overwhelmed by the happiness, Lisa jumped and shouted before her teammates rushed to her and lifted her like a treasure.

Hannah's heart galloped from elation, and she put her fingers in her mouth, whistling out loud. Lisa laughed and came down from her teammates' shoulders, walking toward Hannah. Startled, she looked around as if trying to find who Lisa was looking at only to realize it was her. The spectators' eyes followed her as Lisa walked up to Hannah and grabbed her face, kissing her. Hannah heard claps and cheers around. As Lisa leaned back, Hannah's discerned beaming faces - it wasn't smiles of sarcasm or scowl but genuine happiness.

"It's because of you that we won," Lisa whispered as everyone kept on applauding.

"Why?" Hannah asked, glancing around.

"Because you're here, right beside me, supporting me," Lisa replied. "That's enough for me to overcome any obstacle."

Lisa kissed Hannah again and smiled as phones continued clicking, taking their photos. Hannah realized what Lisa had done - she had told the whole world that she loved Hannah.

*

The leaves had begun turning orange, slowly falling on the ground. As the sunlight hit them, they started sparkling in red. Lisa and Hannah sat under the tree, holding hands and quietly chatting. Lisa's eyes lingered on Hannah's face as the shine retreated behind the wide branches.

Lisa brushed her palm against Hannah's, and she put her

head on Lisa's shoulder. Calmness had taken over the couple as they watched the autumn leaves fluttering in the air. A smile began dancing on Lisa's lips.

"It's so pretty," Hannah murmured as if reading her thoughts.

They heard the sound of footsteps and the fallen leaves crunching under them. Looking up, Lisa saw Gemma, her teammate, approaching.

"Hey!" the girl greeted with a smile.

"Hi," Lisa and Hannah replied.

Gemma flopped next to them on the chair, her eyes sneaking toward the couple, unable to hide the curiosity.

"You played so well last week," Hannah mentioned as Lisa kept tightly holding her hand.

"Thanks," Gemma nodded.

Standing up, Hannah slid her hands down her sleeveless shirt.

"I'm gonna buy some coffee," she said. "Do you want some?"

"No, thanks," Lisa smiled. Gemma shook her head too.

"Okay, I'll be right back." Hannah leaned in, kissing Lisa. She gazed at her before Hannah disappeared in a coffee shop across the street.

"Can I ask you something?" Gemma's voice made her head turn around.

"Yes?"

"What do you see in Hannah?"

A peaceful smile spread across Lisa's face.

"She's the most loyal friend I've ever had," she said. "Her heart is so big and full of kindness. I feel at home when I'm with her."

"What about men?" Gemma asked.

"I don't need any men," Lisa chuckled. "No men can make me feel as happy as Hannah can."

Lisa looked at the street, watching Hannah returning with a cup of coffee in her hand, a broad smile, and love sating her eyes. Lisa felt warmth pouring into her, growing roots in her soul.

The words slipped out of her mouth, said from the bottom of her heart.

"The world is beautiful when I'm with Hannah."

9 798743 555567